Caugh...

She threw herself down in front of her dressing table, leaned her face in her hands, and stared at her reflection.

'He shouldn't be allowed out,' she mouthed. 'He should be branded with a health-risk warning. Oh, *God*, he's gorgeous. I love the way he moves – when he dances on stage, and I love when he hardly moves at all, the way he just lounges in a chair, as if he's so relaxed with himself. I love his voice, I love the way he laughs, the way his eyes crease up when he laughs, that lopsided smile he's got ... And *oh God*, when he gets hold of me, when he kisses me, when we dance, I'm going to pass out with it one day, it's too much, he's gorgeous, Sean's *gorgeous*.'

J-17

Caught In The Act

Just Seventeen

Too Cool To Care
New Place, New Face
Playing Away
Caught In The Act
Triple Trouble
The Red-Hot Love Hunt
Too Hot To Handle
Double-Cross Dilemma
Love Games
Girls On Tour

Caught In The Act

by Kate Cann

RED FOX

A Red Fox Book

Published by Random House Children's Books
20 Vauxhall Bridge Road, London SW1V 2SA

A division of Random House UK Ltd
London Melbourne Sydney Auckland
Johannesburg and agencies throughout the world

Copyright © Random House Children's Books 1997

1 3 5 7 9 10 8 6 4 2

First published in Great Britain by Red Fox 1997

This book is sold subject to the condition that it shall
not, by way of trade or otherwise, be lent, resold,
hired out, or otherwise circulated without the
publisher's prior consent in any form of binding or
cover other than that in which it is published and
without a similar condition including this condition
being imposed on the subsequent purchaser.

The right of Kate Cann to be identified as the
author of this work has been
asserted by her in accordance with the
Copyright, Designs and Patents Act, 1988.

Typeset in Sabon by
Palimpsest Book Production Limited,
Polmont, Stirlingshire

Printed and bound in Great Britain by
Cox & Wyman Ltd, Reading, Berkshire

Papers used by Random House UK Limited are natural,
recyclable products made from wood grown in sustainable
forests. The manufacturing processes conform to the
environmental regulations of the country of origin.

RANDOM HOUSE UK Limited Reg. No. 954009

ISBN 0 09 926318 1

♥

Curtain Up

Aisha threw her bag into a corner of Philly's living room, chucked her coat after it, and fell on the sofa. 'I'm knackered,' she groaned. 'Three hours non-stop rehearsal. Trying to look like I'm in love with that jerk Joel the whole time. D'you realise the effort that takes?'

'Yep. Superhuman,' said Philly, collapsing beside her.

'Well, don't ask me for sympathy,' put in Tasha, squeezing on the end of the sofa. 'I've been sewing stupid glittery wigs all day.'

'I saw them,' said Philly. 'They looked fantastic. Are they for my scene? Beauty School Drop Out?'

'Yeah,' grumbled Tasha. 'And it can drop *right* out as far as I'm concerned. My hands look like they've been grated.'

'Oh, stop moaning,' said Aisha. 'You wanted to be in charge of costumes.'

'Well, *you* wanted to be leading lady.'

'Yeah, but not opposite Joel. If he was any more up himself he'd turn inside out. He's such a pain.'

'Can't you just ignore him?'

'*Ignore* him? Tasha, I have to spend half my life mauling him. I can't take any more.'

'Well, *I* can't take any more cutting and stitching and . . .'

'God, you *miseries*!' exploded Philly. 'It's all worth it. It's going to be brilliant. It's going to be the best production of *Grease* the world has ever seen.'

'Maybe,' grunted Tasha. 'Right now I'm too tired to care. And I'm starving. And dehydrated. Who's going to get the drinks?'

'That's all the way to the fridge,' moaned Aisha. 'You go.'

'No. You.'

'Philly – it's your house. Come on. We're guests.'

'Uninvited!'

'Go on. Philly. Please.'

There was a silence as all three girls settled deeper into the sofa. Finally Philly staggered to her feet and stomped off to the kitchen. She came back with three cans of lemonade and three bags of crisps, saying, 'Here you are, you lazy cows.'

'Lifesaver Award to Phillippa Howard,' said Aisha gratefully, reaching for her share. 'Thanks, Philly.'

'Yeah, thanks,' said Tasha, crunching furiously. 'Oh, that's better. Nourishment. Liquid. And I guess my wigs do look OK, even if my hands will never be the same again.'

'They looked fantastic,' said Philly. 'And that's the last time I'm telling you.'

'So, what d'you think of the new girl?' asked Aisha suddenly.

'Ness? Far too pretty. Hate her,' said Tasha.

'She's all right,' said Philly firmly. 'I think she's fitted in brilliantly. I mean – it's no joke, coming into a production half-way through. It's no joke coming to a college half-way through.'

'Philly, you're always so *fair*. And positive. It's dead irritating. What I mean is – is she as good as Jan?'

Philly rolled her eyes skyward. 'She's better,' she said, 'and you know it.'

'Yeah well – this glandular fever thing, it must have been dragging Jan down these last weeks – her voice had gone, and . . .'

'Aisha, Ness is a better actress than Jan will ever be. With or without glandular fever. Everything's taken off since she took over as Rizzo.'

'She's perfect for Rizzo,' agreed Tasha.

'Some compliment,' Aisha muttered. 'Rizzo's a queen-bitch slapper with a smoking problem. And yeah – Ness *is* good as her.'

Tasha burst out laughing. 'Oh dear. We're not likely to get any objective criticism from you, are we, *darling*? What's the matter? Feeling a little upstaged?'

'No,' retorted Aisha, glaring.

'OK, then – you're jealous because Ness has to snog loverboy on stage, and she really puts herself into it. You're scared Sean'll get blown away and realize what he's been missing for the last six months, give you the heave-ho and . . .' Tasha broke off with a squeal as a cushion landed in her face. Laughing, she lobbed it back at Aisha.

'You're not really jealous of Ness are you, Aisha?' asked Philly, all concern. 'You can't be. Sean's mad on you. He wouldn't even look at anyone else. Everyone knows that.'

'Da-da-dada,' intoned Tasha, singing the Wedding March. 'Da-da- da*da* . . .'

'Tasha, I'm *warning* you – No, Philly. I'm not jealous. I feel so secure with Sean I . . .'

'What?'

'Oh, nothing. I feel very secure, that's all. And Ness is fine. It's just – I mean, she throws herself around so much.'

'She's got energy.'

'Yeah, but there's no need to spew it over everyone so much, is there? That last dance scene with Sean – she nearly went into orbit.'

'Oh, Aisha,' said Philly, giving her a friendly shove, 'leave it *out*.'

The girls stayed motionless on the sofa for a while, chatting about the rehearsal, watching the early evening soaps on the TV and gratefully accepting Philly's mum's offer of a sandwich. Then at about seven, Aisha and Tasha heaved themselves to their feet, slipped reluctantly out into the dark, wintry streets and plodded home.

Aisha let herself into her house, staggered upstairs

and flopped back onto her bed. Slowly, she pulled the band off her long, blonde hair, letting it fall loose and heavy over the pillow. Then she put her arms behind her head and gazed up at the ceiling where she'd taped a large photo of Sean. He looked down at her, grinning, one corner peeling off. He had sandy hair and a great smile, with grey-blue eyes and a mouth that was made to be on the move.

It was their six-month anniversary in a week's time. Six months since that amazing party when they'd finally got together after weeks of eyeing each other in the college canteen and walking slowly past each other in the corridors.

You're a looker, all right, she thought, staring up at him. You're a real looker. And you belong to me. She closed her eyes and thought about the way he said her name whenever they met up, always pleased and somehow surprised, as though he couldn't get over the fact that they were an item. She thought about the way he got her by the elbows and pulled her in close and kissed her. She told herself how nice it was, never having to wonder what you were doing at the weekends, always having someone to go to clubs and parties with, always having someone there at the end of the phone.

'I am so lucky,' she whispered up at the photo. 'I've got you, and I've got the lead in *Grease*, and everything's going right for me.'

Then she rolled over onto her side and sighed, as though something inside her wasn't convinced.

♥

Sporty Boys

Rehearsals started at ten sharp the next morning for the boys in the cast. They were running through one of the fast numbers and working on the choreography. The girls had been told to turn up at twelve to do the café scene, but Aisha and Philly drifted in around eleven. They wanted to see how the lads were doing.

The two girls found themselves a seat at the side of the drama studio and settled down to watch. Music was pounding out so loudly it made the air vibrate. Up on stage, Sean, Ian, Charley and Joel were lined up, learning the steps.

'Sean – ease it off a bit!' yelled the director, Bill. 'I know I said I wanted it raunchy, but those hip movements are obscene!'

Aisha laughed as Sean mimed an even more

obscene movement at Bill's back and then waved to her, a big smile splitting his face. 'He'll be worse now you're here,' grinned Philly.

'OK,' shouted Bill. 'One more time. From the top. And remember – it takes *discipline* to move like a bunch of kids who don't know what the word discipline means – and not end up in a heap on the floor, OK? GO!'

'God,' said Aisha. 'Why does Bill have to be such an idiot. He's so over the top.'

'I know,' said Philly. 'All that "hey – I'm one of you guys" stuff. It's embarrassing. Blimey – look at them go!'

The dance routine the boys had worked out needed all their skill and energy. They jumped in the stage car, they jumped out, they threw each other about – and all the time they were singing, loudly. It looked like chaos, but each movement had to fit the main pattern, so timing was crucial.

'Look at them all,' breathed Aisha. 'Just watch Ian move.'

'Who d'you think I'm watching?' hissed Philly. 'Yes! He did it. He's been practising that back flip all week.'

'Must have been fun for you.'

'It was OK. Jesus – Charley nearly crashed off the stage then.'

'Joel's out of place. Again. Look – he's thrown them.'

'I love this number,' said Philly happily, nodding her head to the beat. 'It's corny, but I love it.'

'Hey – *HI!*' came a shrill voice from behind them.

'Oh God, what does she want?' grumbled Aisha.

'Have the new chorus guys turned up yet?' the shrill voice continued.

'There's your answer,' smirked Philly. 'That's what she wants. *Hi*, Karina. Come to watch?'

Karina was blonde, voluptuous and voracious for new talent. Male talent. She plumped herself down beside Aisha and Philly. 'Oh, it's just that lot still,' she said dismissively, eyeing the stage with distaste. 'Bill said he was bringing in some more guys just to fill out the scene, you know, at the back.'

'Yeah, he is,' said Aisha. 'Real rough types. He wants authenticity.'

Karina brightened. 'He does?'

'Yeah. One of them's six-six, apparently. Muscles like Schwarzenegger.'

'*Yeah?*'

'Scars all up his arms, one ear missing . . .'

'Oh, shut up, Aisha,' Karina complained. 'You're always taking the piss. It really gets on my nerves.' She glared at Aisha with hostility.

Karina played Marty in the show, and still hadn't got over Aisha being given the lead instead of her.

'I think he's got three guys lined up,' said Philly. 'God knows how he got hold of them.'

'Ah, it'd be no problem, luring them in,' said Aisha. 'The drama department is famous for its female talent.'

Philly laughed. 'Too right. Anyway – they're here. We're going to have some serious moving going on for the big dance sequences now.'

'Mmmm,' breathed Karina. 'Sounds *good*.'

'Tasha's got her hands on them at the moment, in the green room. Trying to turn their number threes into fifties quiffs.'

Karina scrambled to her feet, scooping up her bag from the floor.

'Off to the green room, Karina?' laughed Aisha.

'I need Tasha to take my skirt in,' she shrieked back over her shoulder. 'I've just been losing *so* much *weight*.'

'Pass, the sick bag,' groaned Aisha as, up on stage, Bill called a break. Sean and Ian jumped down and headed for their girlfriends. Aisha smiled as the two boys loped towards them. They moved well, like dancers – supple and powerful. They were both great looking guys, Ian a bit shorter than Sean, and much darker – perfect for Philly with her cropped, white-blonde hair. When the four of them went out together, people turned to stare at them.

'Hey, Aisha,' said Sean, coming to a halt in front of her. He was still panting from the dance routine.

Aisha stood up and moved forward to give him a hug. His back felt hot and damp from all the exercise and she could see sweat running down his neck. 'You need a shower, mate,' she said, wrinkling her nose, and he laughed and grabbed her. She slotted under his arm so naturally now, so smoothly, as though they'd been made to fit together.

'That was all right, that routine,' she said. 'You looked good up there. It's coming together, isn't it?'

'Think so,' said Sean. 'God knows what'll happen when we get the beef up there with us though. We're bumping into each other all the time as it is.'

'Have you met them yet?'

'Yeah. They seemed OK. Seemed to think it was all a big laugh.'

Ian raised his head from a lengthy hello kiss with Philly. 'Joel can't understand it. Can't see why they're needed. Mind you – he'd like the whole thing as a solo.'

Sean laughed. 'Yeah. He was saying to me how he never knew what to do in all the gaps. I told him I thought it was pretty tight production – turns out he meant the gaps when he wasn't speaking!'

'Oh, Sean,' said Aisha impatiently. 'He's not that bad.'

'He is,' said Philly. 'Anyway. Are you guys free after this next session?'

'Yep,' said Ian. 'I've had it up to here.' He put

his arm round Philly, pulling her in close. 'Go back to your place? I'm only two weeks late on that economics assignment. One more night won't make any difference.'

Philly put her arms round his chest and squeezed him hard, looking mockingly up into his face. She loved the way he always gave in to temptation – especially when it involved her. 'It's so tough being a stage star *and* still be expected to work, isn't it?' she said.

'Really tough.'

'OK. What about the pub tonight?'

'Yeah. Then we could get a Chinese,' said Ian. 'It's a real laugh, watching you try to eat with chopsticks.' Philly smiled, and hugged him a lot tighter. 'Ouch. What about you two?' he added, turning to Aisha and Sean.

Sean smiled down at Aisha. 'Sound good to you?' he said.

Aisha smiled back, nodding, feigning enthusiasm. And the words came into her head: How cosy. A foursome. *Again*.

'All right, you slackers, back on stage!' yelled Bill. 'I want you four – and Charley and Joel.

Where's Ness? Isn't she here yet? We'll have to go without her.'

Ness was standing in the girls' toilets, gripping the edge of the basin, staring at her face in the mirror, trying to turn herself in to Rizzo. First she had to slow her breathing right down and clear her head of all the shrieking fear and jangling worries and self-doubt. She needed a calm, clear space in there, to let Rizzo in. Only then could she walk out and face everyone.

In the green room, Tasha was trying to keep her cool under pressure. She was penned in by large, well-muscled males. One was seated in front of her, duplicated by the mirror, and two more were standing on either side of her. They had their arms folded and they were leaning towards her, watching her every move.

The mirror reflection frowned as she tugged hopelessly at its hair, trying to make it quiff upwards. 'Maybe it'll be OK,' she said doubtfully.

'I mean – you'd never be able to grow it in time, would you? And some blokes in the fifties had crew cuts. Only I think the ones that did were all in the army.' Oh, *God*, Tasha, stop whittering, she thought.

'But we're not meant to be soldiers, right?' said the guy to her left.

Great grasp of the script, she thought, wondering how to answer that – then she was saved by Karina bounding through the door.

'This skirt is *huge* on me,' shrieked Karina, 'it practically *falls off* – oh *hi* guys!'

'Hi,' said the three sporty boys, in deep unison.

'I'm Karina,' she gushed. 'I play Marty. And you're . . . ?'

'Dave.'

'Chris.'

'Andy.'

'We fill up the background in the dance scenes,' Chris said.

'I bet you do! Fan*tastic*. Have you rehearsed yet?'

'We haven't even learnt the basic steps yet,' said Dave. 'We're sp'osed to be in the gym . . .'

♥ 16 ♥

he checked his watch. 'Christ! Fifteen minutes ago.'

'You'd better go,' said Tasha hastily. 'I've done my bit.'

'I was thinking,' said Chris. 'What about sideburns? I can grow them really quickly.'

'Ooooh, can you?' said Karina.

'Good idea,' said Tasha. 'You need to look kind of . . . sleazy.'

'No problem for Chris, that,' laughed Andy. 'Sleaze is his middle name.'

'Oh really? said Karina, coy as hell. 'Why's that, then?'

There was a silence, during which everyone but Karina looked embarrassed. 'What gear d'we have to wear?' Andy asked.

'Oh, jeans and white T-shirts,' said Tasha. 'And you'll just need basic stage makeup.'

This caused loud laughter and the usual run of *ooh-sweety* comments from the three lads as Tasha opened the door and ushered them out.

Karina collapsed petulantly into the chair that Chris had just vacated. 'What d'you have to sling them out so soon for?' she grumbled.

'I didn't. You heard them – they had to get to the gym.'

'Well, you didn't have to remind them.'

'Yes I did. I had to get them out before you got completely embarrassing. You're like something out of a *Carry On* film sometimes, Karina, I swear. And this skirt is fine on you. If anything, it's tight.'

'Oh, lighten up. I just wanted a reason to come and see you.'

'See *me*? Sure it was me!'

Karina shrugged happily. 'Who cares. That Chris guy was lush. You're *sooo* lucky, getting to tart up all these guys, stripping off their shirts, measuring their inside legs . . .'

Tasha grinned. 'Yeah, well. I need some compensations in this job.'

'So – which one did you go for?'

'I didn't. Not my type.'

'None of them?' Karina was incredulous. 'You're joking. They were all so *fit*. You know what your problem is, Tasha? You're far too choosy. Mind you . . .' and she sneered sideways at Tasha, 'I suppose you do have very distinctive taste.'

This was a comment on Tasha's style. She had richly coloured, wavy hair that she wore differently every day. She liked experimental makeup. She wore three earrings in one ear and one in the other. And she *never* bought her clothes from high-street stores.

'I'm an art student,' said Tasha drily. 'I have to look like this. It's in the contract.'

'Oh, ha ha. Hey – can anyone go to the gym? Only I was thinking – I wouldn't mind starting a weights programme. Just to tone up, you know.'

'Karina,' Tasha groaned, 'why don't you just go and look up the word 'subtle' in the dictionary – and then try to *be* it a bit more?'

Karina smirked and tossed her blonde hair back from her face. 'No one ever got anywhere good by being subtle,' she retorted – and left.

♥

Minefield

'Sorry I'm late,' Ness called out from the back of the hall. She was speaking in the voice she used for Rizzo – gravelly, confident, a bit aggressive.

'OK,' said Bill. 'Try to make it on time next time, OK? We're just getting to you now.'

Ness walked up to the steps, aware that everyone was staring at her. Not with hostility – but just the staring was daunting enough. 'People are bound to stare,' she said to herself. 'You waltz right into a starring role in your second week here – and you attract attention. Just use it, work it, use it for yourself.'

She strutted onto the stage, forcing herself to be brave. A few of the cast smiled and 'Hi-d', and Bill clapped his hands for everyone's attention. 'OK. We've been through this café scene a few times before, and it was good but it's got to be better. It's all on you in this scene, Rizzo. You're the centre. You're scared you might be pregnant – and the way I see it – you're even *more* scared Kenickie might dump you if you are. So what do you do?'

'I dump him first,' said Ness quietly. 'I hurt him before he can hurt me.'

'Good. And Sean – what do you feel? What's going through your mind?'

Sean grimaced. He hated it when Bill started his cheesy method-acting stuff.

'Come on Sean – what do you *feel*?' Bill repeated.

'Well – when she says it's not mine, that's it, right?' muttered Sean. 'I'm so hurt I can't even see straight, right?'

'Right. You're not a subtle guy.'

There was general laughter. Sean and Ness were staring at each other, thinking their way into their characters.

'OK,' said Bill. 'So we need hate and love and fear all mixed up together, Ness. It's a tall order. Let's go from the beginning.'

Aisha's eyes were glued on Ness as she crackled her way through her lines, throwing off anger and need like electric sparks, being somehow hateful and loveable both at the same time. 'OK,' she said to herself, 'I admit it – you can act. You can *really* act.' She could see Sean was charged by Ness's performance, lifted by it. She watched as he grabbed hold of Ness, pulling her against him, making her look at him, face so close to hers they could have kissed. They held that position for a long time, much longer than they'd done before. The passion between them made the air shake, made everyone else on stage fade into the background.

When the scene was finished there was a silence, then Bill shook his head, as though he couldn't quite believe it, and started clapping. 'That was brilliant, kids,' he said, 'you've cracked it. We can't better that. Hold on to it. *Hold on* to whatever you were feeling when you did that scene – it was magic.' He took a deep emotional breath, then beamed round at them all. 'OK – let's break for today.'

'Whooo!' said Philly, as they all clambered down

from the stage, 'that was something else. That got top marks. I've never seen Bill so disgustingly happy about anything.'

Joel glared at Philly. 'You weren't here last Thursday. My reunion scene with Sandy. He said I was superb.'

'Bill doesn't use words like superb, Jo,' said Sean. 'Ever.'

'It's Jo-EL,' Joel snapped. 'Jo-EL. Is that so difficult for you to remember? It's only two syllables, for Chrissake.'

'Sorry, Jo, er . . . Jo-EL. I just don't know why I have a problem with it. Do you, Ian?'

'No idea. It's a great name.'

'Shut *up*,' laughed Philly, whacking Ian on the back.

Joel. He drove everyone up the wall, particularly the girls. They couldn't get over why such a superb physical specimen should be such a total *jerk*. It was such a waste. He had a face carved by an artist, a body fit for a model – and a mind that short-circuited whenever it was asked to consider more than just his own sweet self, self, self.

♥ 23 ♥

'Let's go to the canteen,' said Charley. 'Let's celebrate the star performance.'

'Count me out,' sniffed Joel. 'I have lines to learn. *Some* of us have more lines to learn than others,' and he stalked off.

'What a prima donna,' breathed Ian, as they all watched him go. 'Can't bear the spotlight on anyone else.'

'He's a good-looking bloke,' Ness ventured.

'Don't,' said Philly. 'Don't even think about it, Ness. Aisha'll tell you. She went out with him last year.'

Aisha groaned. 'Oh, thanks, Philly. Shout my crap taste from the rooftops, why don't you. It was before I knew what he was like, Ness. I mean, you're right – he is good looking.'

As she was speaking, Aisha slid her eyes over to look at Ness, taking in her incredible green-brown eyes and mass of auburn hair. Joel isn't the only good looker around here, she thought, ruefully.

'So what happened?' said Ness. 'How long did it last?'

'Two dates,' Aisha said. 'That's all I could stand.

Joel's dad's quite a big actor – he must've told you. He tells everyone.'

'Yeah, he did,' admitted Ness. 'All that stuff about acting being in his blood . . .'

'Right. Well on the second date he took me home and sat me down in front of a video of one of his dad's tired old costume dramas. And while I was watching it, trying to keep awake, his *dad* came in and sat down right next to me on the sofa and started asking me what I thought of it!'

'So that was why the second date was the last date?' asked Ness, laughing.

'That and the fact that he snogs like a sink plunger.'

'I reckon he still fancies you,' said Ian, stirring. 'Those stage kisses aren't just for show.'

'What?' said Sean. 'I'll kill him.'

'Oh, leave it out,' said Aisha. 'I've warned him – any tongue, and I'll knee him. I feel like getting the mouthwash out each time as it is. But he's a bit slow to get the message – I don't think he can believe I'd go for Sean over him.'

'None of us can, Aisha,' said Ian. 'Serious taste lapse there, girl.'

'Yeah, right,' said Sean. 'Very funny. Now come on – let's go and get a drink.' And he put an arm round Aisha's shoulders and steered her towards the canteen, with all the others following, still chatting about the rehearsal and laughing about Joel.

They bought drinks and headed for a table at the side. Ness and Charley sat opposite each other, up against the wall; Sean slid in after Ness and Aisha followed Charley, then Sean reached over and held Aisha's hand across the table.

'Stop luvvy-doveying Aisha and budge up,' said Ian, shoulder barging Sean as he tried to sit next to him. 'Come on. My arse is halfway off the seat.' Sean moved nearer to Ness, but he still left a gap between them, a space.

A space like a minefield, Aisha suddenly thought, a space too dangerous to cross. Why was Sean so scared of sitting near Ness? It was as though all the passion from the scene they'd acted together was still there between them.

Ian attacked his milkshake with a long, drain-like gurgle and said, 'What time are we meeting tonight, Philly?'

'If you keep making disgusting noises like that we're *not* meeting. Ever again.'

'OK. What time?'

'Eight?' said Philly. 'Eight, Sean?'

'Eight OK, Aish?'

Aisha nodded, smiling at him, trying to look enthusiastic. Then she finished her drink. Over the rim of the glass she watched Sean and Ness as they didn't look at each other and didn't touch.

♥

Sean's Gorgeous

Sean and Aisha and Philly and Ian all turned up together at the pub at the same time. They found a free table in the corner and collapsed round it with their drinks and packets of crisps.

'God, it went so well today,' said Sean. 'It was almost worth feeling this knackered for.'

'Almost,' agreed Philly. 'And I'm glad Ness came along with us, after the rehearsal. It was like – I dunno, we hadn't been that friendly before . . .'

'Yeah?' said Ian. 'Well, don't blame Sean and me. I can just imagine the reaction from you girls if we'd been *too* friendly. She's a babe. Joel's on her tracks already. Good job you warned her off, Aish.'

Aisha shrugged. 'It's not up to me to tell her who to go out with. Maybe she fancies him.'

'I don't think so,' Sean said. 'I found her hiding from him the other day, in the props room.'

Aisha looked at Sean, suspicion in her eyes. 'Yeah? Did she say that was what she was doing?'

'Sort of. Well, she said she just went in there for some space, but I saw Joel prowling around outside.'

'Maybe she did just want space. I think she's a bit of a loner.'

Sean shrugged. There was a pause, then Philly stood up. 'Coming to the bog, Aish?' she said.

'Do they synchronise their bladders or something?' grumbled Ian, as the girls headed off.

'Nah,' said Sean. 'They just like to go places in pairs.'

'Weird. Want me to come with you to get the next round in?'

'Yeah, funny. No, I don't.'

'What's up, Aish?' asked Philly, as they leaned across the sinks and examined their faces in the dingy mirror.

'What d'you mean – what's up?' said Aisha.

♥ 29 ♥

'I dunno – you just seem a bit down tonight.'

'Oh – I'm tired. That's all. Why – have I been really boring or something?'

'Well – not exactly a barrel of laughs. Never mind.' Philly spiked her fingers through her hair and turned to grin at her friend. 'Well, how are you going to celebrate it then? And can I come?'

'Celebrate what?'

'You *know* what. Next week – you and Sean have been together six months!'

'Oh, *Philly*,' groaned Aisha. 'How come you remember that?'

'Because I was there when it all started. When you two finally got it together. Oh, it was dead romantic . . .'

'Philly – don't make me *cringe* . . .'

'. . . *and* a huge relief. All you'd *done* up 'til then was whitter on about how fit Sean was but you were too scared to speak to him . . .'

'Christ, was I that bad?'

'Worse. And then that party came along, and the two of you disappeared for ages, and then walked back into the room, hand in hand . . . *Gaaaad*! The start of a perfect relationship.'

'Oh, leave it out,' Aisha snapped.

'Come on, how you going to celebrate? Big party? Hoards of people – loads of nosh?' joked Philly.

'I kind of think it'll be just the two of us, OK?'

'OK. Your loss.'

The girls left the loo and went back to their table. Sean was still at the crowded bar. Philly wrapped her arms round Ian's waist and nuzzled her face into his neck, and then they started chatting about the great party they were going to have once the show was over, a last-night party to end last-night parties. Aisha smiled to herself as she listened to them laughing and flirting together. Philly and Ian had been together for over a year, the original match made in heaven. They're so good together, Aisha thought, they still get such a buzz out of each other. When you listen to them chat, you know the spark's still there.

And suddenly she felt like a cold hand had got hold of her, somewhere deep inside. She looked miserably over at the bar. Sean was standing there, one foot propped on the rail, trying to get the barman's attention. Face it, she thought, it's not like that for me and Sean, not any more. Not like it is for Ian and Philly. I've stopped feeling any sort of spark.

She sighed and looked down at the table. You haven't just had a down patch, she said to herself, or been fed up, or tired, all the things you said to yourself to explain why you never really wanted to kiss him any more . . . why you always pulled away before it went any further . . . why he's been getting on your *nerves* so much lately. You just don't feel hooked on him any more.

She looked sadly over at Philly and Ian, who were talking together, nose to nose. What am I going to do? she thought. I can't just – end it. It'd be horrible. Even thinking it is horrible. How do you tell someone you've just – gone off them? I can't hurt him, I can't. He's such a good bloke. And not so long ago being with Sean was everything, it was all I wanted. Oh, God. *Why* can't that feeling come back?

Ness was stretched full length on her bed, with

the bedroom door barricaded against her two little brothers and her Walkman plugged in against the din of the television downstairs. She subsided into the music, feet moving to the beat, hands behind her head, and realised she felt happy.

The feeling of happiness hadn't been around much since her family had had to up stakes and move right to the other side of the country. At first, she'd missed her old friends so badly she'd felt she was going crazy. Then, when she'd landed the role of Rizzo in the Christmas production, she'd been scared but delighted. Acting meant almost everything to Ness. She was determined to prove herself and today – with that scene with Sean – she was just beginning to think she was pulling it off.

Ness rolled over onto her side, then slid off the bed. She felt restless, energised. Today, she thought, when we went to the canteen – I almost felt part of it. I felt accepted. They're a good crowd. Aisha's brilliant – a bit cool, maybe, but I really like her, and Philly and Ian are dead friendly when they're not stuck to each others' faces.

She sashayed a few steps round the room, nodding her head to the music. Then she threw herself down in front of her dressing table, leaned her face in her hands and stared at her reflection.

'He shouldn't be allowed out,' she mouthed. 'He should be branded with a health warning. Oh, *God*, he's gorgeous. I love the way he moves – when he dances on stage, and I love when he hardly moves at all, the way he just lounges in a chair, as if he's so relaxed with himself. I love his voice, I love the way he laughs, the way his eyes crease up when he laughs, that lopsided smile he's got . . . And, *oh God*, when he gets hold of me, when he kisses me, when we dance, I'm going to pass out with it one day, it's too much, he's gorgeous, Sean's *gorgeous*.'

♥

Frosty!

The next day, Tasha arrived at the green room early with an original Coca-Cola shirt someone's grannie had found up in the attic. Five minutes later Charley turned up to meet her, as arranged.

'Here,' she said, holding the shirt out to him. 'This is why I wanted to see you. It's such a find, Charley. It's authentic fifties.'

Charley looked at it and grimaced. 'Yeah, but it's also seriously tacky. Look at the *collar*. Why do I have to be the one to wear it?'

''Cos Bill's decided Putzy is a bit of a geek, OK? Come on, try it on.'

Grumbling to himself, Charley peeled off his T-shirt and slipped the shirt over his back. 'It's way too tight,' he said, pleased. 'Look – the buttons don't even meet.'

'Charl-*ey*,' remonstrated Tasha. 'Make an effort, can't you? Look – you haven't even got it *on* properly.' She reached up to his shoulders, tugging the shirt material round his chest. 'C'mon – I spent a whole half hour last night mending a tear in it.' She started to do up the buttons.

Charley leaned towards her, letting her hair brush his face. '*Mmmm*,' he said. 'You smell expensive.'

'Yeah? Well, it isn't expensive. Where would I get the money for good perfume from?'

'I dunno. Maybe someone bought it for you.'

Tasha shook her head and carried on fastening up the buttons. 'I can always move these over a couple of centimetres,' she said, 'give you a bit more space.' Just as she got to his navel, Charley grabbed her hands, pressing them up against him.

'Don't,' he said, 'I'm ticklish down there.'

'OK, you do it then. C'mon, Charley, let go of my hands.'

'Come out with me, Tasha,' he said, pulling her closer. 'Go on. Just one date.'

'Charley, we've been through this.'

'But how can one date hurt?'

'No. I told you. I just want to be friends. Now come on. Let go.' But she didn't pull her hands away. It felt good, pressing her hands to his stomach, feeling the muscles there, the tension in them. It's so long, she thought, since I've been held by a boy. Since I've been kissed. Then this desire to just reach up and kiss Charley came over her and she pulled away from him, abruptly.

'Whooo,' Charley said. 'Frosty.'

'Oh shut up,' Tasha snapped. 'Why do blokes always say stuff like that when girls don't fall at their feet?'

'Hey, calm down. I was only joking. I just think we'd have a good time together, Tasha, that's all. I think you'd enjoy yourself. I mean – what are you saving yourself up for?'

Then he unbuttoned the Coca-Cola shirt in silence, took it off and threw it on a chair, put on his T-shirt and left the green room, looking sulky.

He's right, thought Tasha, what *am* I saving myself up for? Charley's a nice guy. He's funny, sweet . . . She sighed and picked up the shirt

Charley had discarded, smoothed out the creases and hung it on a hanger. Maybe old happy-slappy Karina's right, she thought. Maybe I *am* far too choosy.

In the drama studio, rehearsals were in full swing. Everyone knew that things had shifted up a gear. The countdown had started; there were less than three weeks to go now until opening night. Bill went into panic overdrive, working everyone really hard all morning. He wasn't a bit satisfied with Joel and Aisha's love scene at the drive-in.

'Come on Aisha,' he said, 'put a bit more into it. You're completely *bonkers* about this guy. The attraction's so strong it's broken through all your prejudices about boys like him.'

Joel smirked in her direction and flicked back his perfectly cut hair. It'd take more than attraction to break through my prejudices about him Aisha thought sourly. She stomped back to the wings to make her entrance again, muttering about it taking more than just talent to act like you were mad on Joel.

Five minutes into the scene, Bill sent her back to the wings again. 'Come *on*, Aisha,' he said. 'You look like you're kissing your grandma. Give me some passion, can't you?'

Aisha scowled and headed once more for the side of the stage. While she waited for her cue, she noticed Sean and Ness chatting at the side of the hall. Plenty of passion going on there, she thought uneasily. *Great* body signals. She watched Ness throw back her head and laugh. Ness couldn't seem to keep still on her feet; she was drawing spirals in the air with her hand as she explained something, all happy animation. Sean was laughing too. He had his arms folded, as though he needed to protect himself from something.

This time, Bill let the scene run its full course. He announced he still wasn't satisfied, but it was getting better. Then he told everyone to break for lunch. Aisha jumped down from the stage and joined Sean and Ness. 'Hi,' she said, taking Sean's arm a bit possessively. 'Having fun?'

'It's happened,' Sean said, laughing. 'Joel asked Ness out.'

'Oh, *no*! What did you *say*?'

'*No*, of course! But he couldn't seem to understand it. It was like I was talking in Martian or something. He kept trying to, like, *interpret* what I was saying as a *yes*.'

'He'll think you're really weird now. Or blind,' said Sean.

Ness laughed. 'Or totally lacking in taste – or *gay* – or . . .'

'C'mon, Sean,' interrupted Aisha. 'Let's get lunch. I'm starving.'

'Want to join us?' Sean asked Ness.

'No,' said Ness. 'Er – thanks. I'll see you later, OK.'

Don't worry, Aisha, Ness thought, as the couple swung out of the room, arms round each other. I don't go in for trying to steal other girls' blokes. Anyway, I wouldn't stand a chance. How could I match up to you? I can see how relaxed you are with him, how confident. I can be that as Rizzo – scrape my fingers across his back, get hold of his chin, pull his face round to mine and kiss him. But in real life? That's different. That's totally different.

♥

Serious Second Thoughts

Dave, Chris and Andy, the three sporty lads who'd volunteered to swell out the background in some of the dance scenes, had their first rehearsal with the rest of the cast. It was chaotic and noisy – and a success.

When they'd finished, all the lads jumped down from the stage, laughing and chatting. Immediately, Karina whisked into the middle of them, yelping congratulations. Tasha had wandered by with an armful of clothes and stayed to watch; Andy made a beeline for her and started asking for her opinion on how he'd done. Ness was laughing with Charley; Joel was chatting up two of the chorus girls.

Sean got hold of Aisha's hand and together they stood in silence, watching all the ducking and weaving. *It's like we're kids who can't join* in the fun, thought Aisha, miserably. We have each other, so we're out of the game. And it suddenly hit her how much she really missed all that, the silly, meaningless fun of it, the excitement – flirting and fooling around and just having a laugh.

'Hey, Aisha,' said Philly, wandering over, 'you know that essay you said you'd help me with . . .'

'Did I?' Aisha replied unenthusiastically. 'Oh, yeah. How far have you got?'

'The opening line?'

'Oh, *Philly*.'

'It's a good line! Honestly, it's a *great* line. But I've got no idea how to continue. I've done the research, honestly Aish, but I've got writer's thingy – you know, block. Serious writer's block. And I thought if you wouldn't mind . . .'

Aisha's mind drifted off as Philly tried to talk her into helping her out. Sean had slipped her hand and had gone to join Ness and Charley. She watched him walk up to them: from the minute he joined them, it was as if Charley was sidelined. Out of the picture. Sean stood right in front of Ness, close, and she turned all her attention to him, and Aisha, watching, had this sense of an energy field between them, communicating all sorts of unspoken things.

Sean and Ness started laughing together, really cracking up over something Sean had said. Sean put his hand on Ness's arm, as if he might fall over if he didn't have someone to support him, and Ness's eyes were wide and wild and fixed on his face.

And Aisha felt the cold hand again, pressing down on her. Face it, Aisha, she thought, we never have fun like that any more. Never. If I had the guts, I'd finish it, only I'm scared that'll make me feel worse. Then she turned away, depressed.

'OK, kids, listen up,' said Bill loudly, coming to the front of the stage and clapping his hands. 'We have a lighting boy at last. I'd better introduce you to him.' He spun round and shouted towards the back of the stage, 'Aidan! Aidan? You back there? C'mere a minute will you?'

There was a long pause, then a bad-tempered thud, as though someone had dropped something heavy on the ground from a great height. Then Aidan appeared through the curtains.

He was black, about six foot two, long, long

legs, broad shoulders. Expressionless face, carved, symmetrical, perfect. Strong nose, strong chin, deep, deep, dark eyes.

For at least five seconds, Tasha forgot to breathe. *He's the one*, she thought, half in delight and half in sheer panic. *He's the one I've been waiting for* . . .

Karina had been smitten by a similar affliction. She goggled at Aidan, open-mouthed, and then she giggled.

'This is Aidan,' said Bill, in a matter of fact tone. 'He's doing art and he's a genius with lighting – he's already come up with some good ideas for the show. So help him out when you can, guys, OK? He's going to be around a lot in the next couple of weeks. Right, Aidan?'

'Right,' said Aidan. 'I s'pose.'

He had a deep, dark voice, all soft and resonant. When she heard it, Tasha sighed with yearning. Karina clutched the arm of the girl standing next to her and mock-swooned. Aidan gave one long, expressionless look at the group in front of the stage, then he turned silently on his heel and stalked off, back behind the stage curtain.

'Blimey,' said Sean. 'What's his problem?'

'Dunno,' said Ian. 'Having to work with Bill?'

'Maybe. He's got a real chip on his shoulder about something.'

'Chip on his shoulder?' put in Joel. 'He could supply *McDonald's*.' He went off into a peal of self-satisfied laughter.

Sean turned to look at Joel. 'That joke doesn't really work,' he said. 'They're called fries in McDonald's, not chips.'

'And it makes it even *less* funny when *you* laugh at it,' added Charley. 'It kind of makes the fact that no one else is laughing a lot more obvious.'

'Not planning on a career as a stand-up comedian, are you mate?' said Ian. 'Stick to straight.'

Joel spun on his heel, swung his bag angrily over his shoulder and stomped out of the hall

'No offence, Jojo!' Sean shouted after him.

'Aw,' said Philly. 'I could almost feel sorry for him.'

'Don't bother,' said Ian. 'He's been really pissing us off. You try dancing next to him. It's a nightmare.'

'The only good bit today,' added Sean, 'was when Chris put him out of action for half an hour by landing on his foot.'

'By accident?' Philly gasped.

Ian shrugged. 'Who cares?'

Who indeed? thought Tasha, as she floated back to the green room. Right now she didn't care about anything, anything at all, but getting another glimpse of Aidan. If he's doing art, how come I haven't seen him before? she wondered. Someone that completely, breathtakingly fabulous doesn't just blend into the crowd. Just where has he been hiding?

'Come on girls,' shouted Bill from the stage. 'Let's have one more run through of the dreaded sleepover scene. Full bitch mode, OK?'

Sean and Ian watched as the Pink Ladies and Sandy clambered back on the boards. 'This scene gives me the shivers,' muttered Sean. 'D'you think they're really like that – on their own I mean?'

Ian laughed. 'We'll never know.'

'We could bug one of their bedrooms.'

'I think I prefer not knowing.'

'Yeah. Maybe you're right.'

There was a silence. 'So,' said Ian, 'what are you getting Aisha for your six-months' thing then?'

'What?'

'You could get jewellery. Girls really like that. A necklace or something.'

'Hmm. Earrings, maybe. She's had her ears pierced again.'

'Yeah – earrings'd be good.'

There was a pause. 'And?' said Ian.

'And – what?'

'What are you going to do to celebrate?'

'Oh, for God's sake. I dunno. Nothing.'

'That'll be fun. Aisha'll really know where she stands then.'

Sean looked up, annoyed. 'What're you saying?'

'Oh, work it out Sean,' Ian snapped. 'You'd have to be stupid not to see what's going on.'

Sean lowered his head and glared at the floor. There was a burst of music from the stage. Ness was belting out her 'Sandra Dee' song, all mockery and exaggeration.

'It's her, isn't it,' said Ian.

Sean shook his head, as if to shake something away. 'Oh, God,' he burst out. 'She's – she's so – she's – I don't know. Look at her. She's gorgeous. She blows me away. Oh, God, I don't know. I don't know what to *do*.'

♥

Lights, Action

When the scene was over, Ness smiled patiently as Bill gushed out congratulations on her song, then she hurried from the stage, calling out an excuse about having to get home quickly to babysit her little brothers.

'You're going to blow it, Ness,' she muttered to herself as she raced away, 'you're really going to blow it if you don't watch it. Why d'you have to go and get the hots for him, you idiot? You were just beginning to feel part of the group – and now this happens. Aisha's hardly going to want to chum up with someone who's after her bloke. She probably thinks there's something going on already, the way we . . . the way we . . . what *is* going on anyway? Does he have any *idea* what I'm feeling?'

* * *

News of Aidan's arrival had spread like wildfire through the girls in the cast; it seemed he was all anyone could talk about. Groups of girls hung out backstage just on the off-chance he'd slope by; they'd stare fixedly as he climbed up and down his ladder; and they'd sit in huddles in the canteen, discussing him. His long legs, his broad shoulders, his gorgeous face, the way he moved, his total air of mystery. No one had seen him smile and no one had yet got him to open his mouth, but this just strengthened his appeal.

Tasha didn't like being part of a fan club, especially one with Karina as a leading member, but she had to admit she was as hooked as the rest of them. She had only to catch sight of him and her heart speeded up. She'd met Aisha for lunch and talked of nothing else but Aidan for the whole hour, leaving Aisha really amazed, because Tasha had a real reputation for being impossible to please as far as guys went.

'You mean there's *nothing* wrong with him?' Aisha had asked, incredulous. 'Nothing you'd change at all?'

'Nothing,' Tasha had said mournfully. 'It's an obsession, Aish. It's eating me up.'

And as if being eaten up wasn't enough, she was having big problems with the costumes, too. She wanted to go really over the top with the 'Beauty School Drop Out' scene, but the boy playing the Teen Angel said he couldn't move in the Elvis-style shirt she'd designed for him. They'd met to work out a compromise but it had practically ended in a fist fight. Tasha had wound up yelling abuse and telling him to make his own damn costume. Then she stormed back to the green room, dumped the costume and locked up for the night.

'I've had it with this place, and this stupid play,' she grumbled to herself, as she stomped along behind the stage to the exit. 'You get no thanks, no gratitude, no acknowledgement that you're giving up *all* your free time . . .'

Suddenly a pair of very long, jeans-clad legs swung down in front of her face and Aidan dropped like a vampire from the rafters, landing on his hunkers right next to her.

It was a completely thrilling appearance. It so shocked Tasha she couldn't breath for a second or two.

'Sorry,' he grinned, standing up straight. 'I dropped

my screwdriver.' He bent to pick it up off the floor. 'You were looking like I feel, girl. What's up?'

'What's –? Oh. I – er – I just had a row with someone.'

'Boyfriend?'

'Oh . . . no . . . someone I've made a costume for. He hates it. Says he can't move in it.'

Aidan shook his head. 'Typical. Actors. It's all ego with actors. I hate 'em.'

Tasha laughed, delighted. 'Yeah, me too. Well, right now, anyway.'

'They don't see broader than their own selves. All those big egos, up on the stage together, banging into each other. It stinks.'

'Yeah. I mean – I wouldn't have minded so much if I hadn't spent so *long* on it. But he just chucked it aside like a – like a *rag*.'

Aidan shook his head. 'It's like all that counts is their performance. They don't rate what anyone else does.'

'Yeah. Anyway.' She cast her mind frantically around for some more conversation. Anything to keep this fantastic creature in her line of vision a bit longer. 'How're you getting on with the lighting?'

'OK. But they won't let me do anything interesting with it. I had this great idea, this grim lighting, for one of the sad scenes – and that dark-haired guy, that Joel?'

Tasha groaned. 'I know him. Biggest ego of the lot.'

'He said it made his face look sallow. Jesus. He was checking in this mirror on the side of the stage – I couldn't believe it. I told him to put more blusher on. He didn't like that either.'

'No, he wouldn't.'

There was a pause. Tasha could feel her blood racing. 'Well' said Aidan. 'I'd better get back up there. Screw in some more 40-watts.'

She laughed and watched him as he turned his back on her and started clambering up the side ladder, hauling himself up with incredible ease. She stared after him, oblivious to anything else, hoping he wouldn't turn round and catch her staring.

He *talked* to me, she thought. He actually opened his mouth and *spoke*. Then she floated out of the drama studio and into the street, high as a helium balloon.

* * *

'It's happened, we've talked, I'm in *love*!' Tasha screeched down the phone to Philly. Then she went over the whole scene she'd had with Aidan, second by second, nuance by nuance, in a non-stop, pleasure-filled monologue. She analysed everything. When he'd said 'You were looking like I feel' it *had* to mean he'd been watching her before he jumped down, it *had* to. Which meant that seeing her had to be *why* he jumped down, it absolutely *had* to. She described in detail the dazzling moment when he'd just dropped out of the rafters and landed beside her. Whoooo, she breathed, remembering the impact it had had on her. Whoooo-*ooooo*.

On the other end of the phone, Philly was enjoying a slow foot massage, courtesy of Ian, and she managed to 'mmmmm' and 'aaaah' with real feeling in almost all the right places. 'So when are you going to ask him out?' she said, when Tasha finally let her get a word in.

'Ask him . . . ?! You've got to be *joking*. I couldn't just *ask him out*.'

'Why not? He's just a guy.'

'Philly,' said Tasha firmly, 'Aidan is not "just a guy". He's – I don't know what he is.'

'A god? A sex hologram? An alien from planet *Lurrvvv?*' suggested Philly, while Ian laughed.

'Get lost, Phillippa Howard. If you're just going to take the piss . . .'

'Aw, Tasha. I'm not. Honest. It's brilliant. *He's* brilliant. I think he definitely fancies you and you should ask him *out!*'

'No. Never. I couldn't. I'd – I'd sooner – I *couldn't*. I mean – if I tried to – I'd – no, I *couldn't*.'

'So what you going to do, then?'

'I don't know. I just don't know. But I have to get him. *Somehow.*'

After ten minutes more of this Philly managed to put the phone down. 'Tasha's found someone she really fancies at last,' she told Ian. 'I've never heard her this blown away about *anyone*. She's really got it bad.'

'Me too,' murmured Ian, moving slowly up Philly's leg.

♥

Girl Talk

The next morning's rehearsals went along at a great pace. Bill announced that they'd really got the whole thing together now and that all that was needed was some ironing out here and there. Then he told them to clear off for an early lunch.

Joel cornered Aisha just as she was disappearing out of the door to fetch her coat. 'Aisha!' he said gushingly, laying a hand on her arm. 'Aisha, we really have to talk.'

'We do?' said Aisha reluctantly.

'Yeah. Our scenes. They're just not as – they're not as *hot* as they should be. I think we need to practise.'

Oh, spare me, thought Aisha. She suddenly felt incredibly weary. 'Well, you know, Joel,' she said, 'I don't know about hot, I'm kind of playing Sandy as *very* virginal, you know? Very reluctant. I mean – I think that's what attracts Danny. Don't you?'

'Well – yes,' said Joel. 'But at the end – when Sandy gets all tarted up – that's when she really comes alive, surely. Physically.'

'Yeah – but she's inexperienced, remember. She's shy. I think it should all be *implied*.'

'But there are more *direct* ways of implying it,' said Joel.

'I'm not sure that makes sense, Joel, does it? Bit of a logic-gap there. You can't say . . .'

'My dad said he'd run through it with us if we wanted,' interrupted Joel. 'Maybe give us a few tips.'

Over my dead body, thought Aisha. 'That's . . . nice of him, but . . .'

'He knows a lot about this kind of acting. How to . . . Well, you saw him in that telly-drama, remember?'

It's etched on my memory with acid, thought Aisha. 'Joel, I really don't think . . .' she began.

'Oh, Aisha. You didn't always find it hard to get passionate with me. Did you?' And he moved closer to her, smiling.

'Look Joel, just cut it out,' said Aisha warningly. 'That was ages ago.'

'Only seven months.'

'Joel, there's nothing between us. You *know* that,' she said, backing away.

'I've changed a lot in those seven months, Aisha,' he replied, following her. 'I've really – *matured*.'

He'd somehow managed to manoeuvre her into the wide space between two sets of lockers in the corridor, blocking her escape route. Oh, blimey, she thought, I'm going to have to smack him one in a minute.

Joel put his arm snakily around her shoulder. 'Come on,' he murmured, 'I'm only talking about an extra rehearsal.'

Aisha pulled away and saw Ness standing there watching them, one hand frozen on her locker door, mouth hanging open.

'Hey – *Ness*,' squawked Aisha. 'Come to find me? I'd forgotten I'd said we'd have lunch. Joel – I'll catch you later. OK? C'mon, Ness.' And she pushed past Joel, grabbed Ness by the arm and towed her along the corridor towards the exit.

'Sorry,' she breathed, as soon as they got outside.

'I had to do that. I had to. He'd started to get all nostalgic about me and – *whoo*. I mean – I could've just kneed him, but that would have made acting opposite him a *bit* difficult – even more gruesome than it is now.'

'It's fine,' said Ness. 'I understand. It's just I thought I was hallucinating when I saw you two together.'

'Yeah, well – I wish you *had* been hallucinating. God, what a slimeball. What a *creep*. Saying he wanted to rehearse the love scene with me. *Urrgh*!'

Ness laughed. 'Well, you handled it brilliantly. Queen of diplomacy.'

'You think? Yeah – maybe you're right.'

'I *am* right. You put the show first. That's just so unbelievably *noble*, Aisha!'

'Totally self-sacrificing, right?' laughed Aisha. 'Anyway – thanks for playing along with it. I am *so* glad you appeared when you did!'

'S'OK. Glad to help out. OK then . . . I'll . . . I'll see you . . .'

'Ness, look – why don't we have lunch anyway? Let's get out of this place, just for an hour or so.'

'Well – yeah . . . OK.'

'Café des Amis, in town. Have you been there? It's great. *And* cheap.'

'OK, I'd love to,' Ness grinned. 'Come on, let's go.'

The two of them hurried out of the college grounds and into the centre of town. Aisha started yakking away about how Joel was so oblivious to the difference between acting and reality he was convinced her smitten onstage act was for real and that was why he'd tried it on again. Ness made her laugh telling her how Joel was still unable to grasp the fact that she, Ness, didn't want to go out with him and how he kept suggesting different places to go and telling her not to be so shy.

'Shy!' said Ness indignantly. 'He really thinks the only reason I've said no is because I'm *shy*!'

'It's really sad, when you think about it,' said Aisha. 'I mean – he's so one-dimensional. Half-dimensional. Can you be half-dimensional?'

'Joel can.'

'He just wants a girlfriend, but it's going to be hard finding someone who thinks as much of him as he does himself. Come to think of it, it's scientifically *impossible*.'

This is weird, Ness thought, as they turned into the café and found an empty table. We're getting on really well together. *Can* you get on really well with the girlfriend of the guy you've fallen for? Aren't there laws about things like that?

The girls ordered open sandwiches and juice and settled down to eat. 'Ness – I'm going to come clean,' Aisha suddenly announced. 'I don't think I was as friendly to you when you first joined the cast as I should've been. And that was totally unfair of me. I mean, you can't help your looks, can you?'

For a moment, Ness looked stricken. 'My . . . ?'

'*Or* the way you act.' Aisha burst out laughing. 'You should see your *face*! Your *good* looks, dummy! And you act brilliantly. You know you do.'

'*Oh*! Er – thanks. So do you. I mean . . .'

'And we have something in common now, right?'

Ness's stomach felt as though it had gone into seizure. 'We *do*?' she whispered.

'Yeah. The honour of having Joel hitting on us.'

'Oh. Right. *Right*!'

'Cheers,' said Aisha, clinking her glass into Ness's.

'Cheers,' Ness replied, relieved. Aisha's great, she

thought. I'd really like her as a friend. No wonder Sean's so into her. Oh, *God*.

'So,' went on Aisha, 'what do you make of the cast then? And are you drooling over the new lighting boy, like everyone else is?'

Ness shrugged. 'Not really. I mean – I can see he's gorgeous, but . . .'

'Gorgeous? He's *sensational*. He must work out five hours a day to get a body like that. Or maybe it's all the clambering about he does, fixing the lights. Everyone's getting in a real state about him, it's amazing. Even Tasha's lost it, and her standards are well high . . . and Karina's just about doing herself in over him.'

'Karina? I thought she was after Chris . . .'

'Karina always has lots of possibilities lined up. She gets through about eight men a week. Well – maybe not eight, but you know.' Aisha shrugged. 'I dunno. I envy her in a way.'

Ness's mouth dropped open. '*You* envy *her*? But you've got – you've got . . .'

'Sean. Yes I know. And he's great. It's just – sometimes I miss really partying, really going wild, you know? I don't mean completely crazy, like

Karina. Just messing around, having some fun.' She leaned over the table to Ness, smiling. 'Hey – you know Dave – the big guy at the back in "Greased Lightning"?'

Ness nodded, wide-eyed.

'I really like the look of him. He's cute. Oh, not for anything serious, just to have a laugh with. Just to get off with at a party and . . . snog each other senseless!' She laughed; then she threw herself back in her chair and sighed. 'I shouldn't be *feeling* this, right? Not when I'm going out with Sean.'

'No, but – you can't help what you feel,' stammered Ness.

'I just – I just feel so *tied down* sometimes,' Aisha almost exploded. 'I feel like I'm standing on the edge, watching it all go by without me. Oh, it was brilliant to start off with, absolutely brilliant, with Sean and me. He was absolutely all I wanted – I even taped his photo to my ceiling, so I could go off to sleep gazing up at him – I mean, besotted or *what*? But the last couple of months it's just been – oh, I don't know. I'm beginning to feel – I feel I want to move . . . I'm – I'm *bored*.'

Under cover of the table, Ness was digging the

nails of one hand into the palm of the other. It was as though she was being given some very precious information – information she didn't quite know what to do with yet.

'He gets on my nerves sometimes like – like – *anything*,' Aisha rattled on. 'I feel such a bitch, but I can't help it, he irritates me, and I snap at him, and – oh, I don't know, we just don't seem to have a laugh any more. It's all got really samey. I used to wait for him to phone as though my life depended on it, and now half the time I'm all, oh God, what does he want again . . . and yet he's so sweet, and we still have good times, it's just . . . *Jesus*, Ness, d'you mind me going on like this?' Aisha said, suddenly, leaning over the table towards her. 'It's just – it's easier sometimes, talking to someone you don't know. Know that well, I mean,' she corrected herself, catching Ness's downward glance.

'No – it's – really, it's fine,' croaked Ness.

'Tasha can't get her brain round anything that isn't Aidan at the moment. And Philly – she just thinks we're perfect for each other. I tried to talk to her the other night and she went on as though feeling like this was something that would just go away – like it was a silly phase I was going through. I mean – to her, splitting up with Sean is completely unthinkable. She said you can't *expect* it to be as exciting six months on as it was at first. Well – I want it to be. I want to feel those goosebumps again!' Then Aisha stopped and looked at Ness, almost in surprise at everything that had just poured out of her.

'It must be awful,' said Ness, with real sympathy.

'It is. I'm really messed up about it.'

Ness made herself meet Aisha's eyes and said, 'And you don't know how he feels?'

'No. But then – I don't suppose he knows how *I* feel. I mean, I don't think I've been acting all that different when I'm around him. I just don't want to *hurt* him. I'm so fond of him. And it's not his fault.'

Ness took a deep breath. 'You should talk to him,' she said. 'You should tell him. It's just not fair not to. Not fair on you or – or him. I'd hate to be with someone who was with me just 'cos they felt sorry for me. I'd *hate* it.'

Aisha looked down at her plate. 'Yeah, I know

you're right. It's just – suppose it really hurts him? I mean – just how *do* you tell someone you've gone off them? It's horrible. It makes me feel sick just to think about telling him. I wouldn't even know where to *start*.'

'Maybe if you start talking,' began Ness, 'maybe you'll find he feels a bit the same. I mean – if the spark's gone, maybe it's gone for both of you.'

Aisha looked up. Her face looked suddenly drained and wan. 'I've got to do it, haven't I?' she said. 'I can't let it go on like this. It's eating me up inside. It's like living a big lie.'

There was a long pause. 'We'd better get back,' said Ness abruptly, checking her watch. 'Look at the time. I've got a class at two.'

The girls left the café and made their way back to college. At the doors, Aisha said goodbye and thanks to Ness, then she stood and watched her as she hurried down the corridor. Well, Aisha, she thought, full of self-amazement, you really let it all hang out then, didn't you? You really let the floodgates open. To the one girl who probably has most interest in Sean being single again. Freudian or *what*?

* * *

Ness didn't go straight to the classroom. She ducked into the girls' toilets and stooped over a basin to splash cold water on her face. Then she dried her skin and looked at her reflection in the mirror. It stared back at her, eyes wide. The conversation she'd had with Aisha had torn her in two. She felt almost hysterical, as though she wanted to cartwheel round the room; she felt guilty and happy and sorry for Aisha and mad with excitement, all at the same time. 'Now what?' she whispered to herself. '*Now* what?'

♥

The Big Break-up

'I mean – he's incredible,' Karina was burbling, sprawled on the old sofa in the green room. 'Like a panther. He's so strong – you should see the way he lifts things, all those heavy lights and things. And he has the best arse in the world.'

Tasha groaned and pulled a box of stage makeup towards her. She was supposed to be sorting it out and making a list of stuff she needed to replace.

'He gave me *the* most seductive look the other day,' Karina droned on. 'I mean – I really think he's noticed me.'

'Yeah?' snapped Tasha, throwing kohl sticks into a tin. 'And what about Chris?'

'Chris? Oh, he's yesterday's. He has nothing like the shape that Aidan has. That guy is gorgeous. He has pecs like I've never *seen*. He has legs that just go *all the way* and . . .'

Something in Tasha cracked. 'You know what, Karina?' she said. 'I'm just about sick of listening to you. You're like some old lech, pulling dirty mags down off the top shelf. You should hear yourself. Cute butt, great pecs, good legs. It makes me want to throw up, it really does.'

'Well, *sorreee*!' said Karina sarcastically. 'I certainly didn't mean to sicken you.'

'You *dissect* them. I mean – you're like some kind of butcher. You think that's all there is to a bloke.'

'I do not!' Karina's eyes were wide with indignation. 'I just appreciate good looking lads. What's the matter, Tasha?' she added nastily. 'Don't you?'

'Yes. But I don't bleat on and on about it, and I don't embarrass them by . . .'

'By what?'

'I saw you! Hanging round right underneath Aidan's ladder, ogling up at him, making all those comments . . .'

'Look – I was just showing my appreciation . . .'

'Yeah? Well, *you're* pretty quick to get snotty if any bloke talks about you that way.'

'Not if it's the right bloke, I'm not.'

'Oh, for heaven's sake. Hasn't it ever occurred to you that people are more than just their *bodies*?'

Karina gawped at her. 'You doing philosophy or something?' she said. 'I thought you were textile art.'

Ness walked into the canteen, saw Sean, Ian and Charley sitting in the corner together and panicked. She cast one look of sheer longing at Sean then she went to the counter and took a long, long time choosing a salad.

'Look who's come in,' said Ian meaningfully.

'I can see her,' said Sean.

'What?' said Charley.

Ness put her salad on a tray, got a drink and paid. She stood looking anywhere but at Sean, then she waved frantically to a girl in a green dress who was sitting on the other side of the canteen. The girl was a bit surprised, because she and Ness had barely spoken to each other before, but they were in the same history group, so she smiled and beckoned Ness to join her.

The three lads watched Ness cross the floor and sit down with her back to them. 'Avoidance tactics,' said Ian, even more meaningfully.

'Look – shut up, you smug git,' said Sean.

'What?' repeated Charley.

'Well, why didn't she sit with us, eh?' went on Ian.

'Maybe your ugly face put her off, mate. Maybe she's heard about Charley's burping problem.'

'Or maybe . . .'

'Look – just *shut it*. You don't know what you're on about.'

'Oh yes I do,' said Ian.

'What's going *on*?' said Charley.

Once Aisha had decided she had to talk to Sean about their relationship going nowhere, she knew she had to get on with it fast, before her courage failed her. She phoned him and arranged to meet him in the pub that night. As she got ready to go she kept rehearsing over and over in her mind what she had to say to him, until the words got jumbled up and senseless and meant nothing.

I wish I could have a script for this one, she thought. I wish I could just say my lines, and he could say his, and it would all be predictable and the curtain would come down and we could go off home and forget it.

She was so nervous by the time she got to the pub she was actually shaking. Sean was already at the bar, with two drinks in front of him. When she came up beside him he smiled and kissed her and gave her one of the drinks. Then he put his arm round her and steered her towards an empty table by an open window. A thin, cold breeze was blowing in from outside. Aisha inhaled it thankfully, hoping it would clear her head.

'So,' said Sean, 'how's things?'

'Fine. I – fine. Bill is *finally* satisfied I'm putting enough passion into my last scene with Joel.'

'Not too much, I hope,' said Sean, in automatic-boyfriend-mode.

'No chance of that. How's your dad? Has he got over his flu yet?'

'Yeah – well, nearly.'

'Still in bed, still driving your mum mad?'

'Yes. Well – he got up to watch the footie last night.'

'Good. That's good. Who was playing?'

'Er – Arsenal. And Tottenham.'

'Right. Good match?'

There was a pause. Suddenly, Sean pushed his chair away from the table and sat back. 'OK, Aisha, what is this?' he said. 'Since when have *we* made small talk?'

'What d'you mean?'

'What did you want to see me about? You sounded dead weird on the phone and you're acting it now.'

Aisha was silent. She looked down wretchedly at the table, twisting her glass round and round in her hands.

'What is it, Aish? What's happened? Come on – you're scaring me.'

At last Aisha found the courage to look up at him. 'Oh. Christ,' she said. 'I don't know what I've come here to say. It's just – it's just – we've been together nearly six months now and – and . . .' Suddenly, Aisha seemed to collapse. Tears started spooling down her face, one after the other, a steady stream of them.

'Aisha, what's *wrong*?' said Sean desperately. He reached over and got hold of her arm, squeezing it. 'What *is* it, Aisha?'

'Oh, Sean, I feel such a cow,' she wailed, dabbing frantically at her eyes. 'You're so sweet, and you're so nice, and – and . . .'

'And what? You're dumping me?' He said this almost teasingly, as though it couldn't be true.

There was a long pause. She glanced up at him miserably.

'Oh,' he said. He looked pale, as though all the blood had suddenly drained from his face.

'It's just not the same any more, Sean,' she whispered. 'Is it?'

'Isn't it?'

'It's not that I don't like you any more. I think you're great. Really great. I'm really fond of you, Sean, honestly. But that's it. It's like you're a friend – a really, really good friend, not a . . . not a . . .'

'Not someone you fancy?'

Aisha took a big breath. 'No. Not any more. I'm *sorry*. It's just got – stale. You must feel that, Sean. You *must* feel it too. We don't even kiss like we used to. Do we?'

Sean was staring down at the table, hard. When he looked up his eyes were wet, too.

'It's like – we spend time together just 'cos we're *together*,' Aisha rushed on, as though she could somehow talk away the pain, 'just 'cos we're a *couple* and the thing is, I don't always want to *be* that, not deep down.'

'I liked it,' said Sean. 'I liked being a couple with you. I really liked it, Aish.'

Aisha started crying again and got hold of his hand. 'Oh, Sean, so did I. But – but – don't you think it's time to move on? Don't *you* ever feel you want to break out a bit, flirt a bit, do something with someone else?'

Sean looked away from Aisha, and Ness's green-brown eyes and mass of auburn hair passed slowly behind his eyes. 'Yeah,' he said, a bit guiltily. 'I guess. Sometimes.'

'I still like you,' she repeated, 'such a lot. But I find myself looking at other guys and feeling a bit tied down and – and it's not *fair* to be with you when I feel like that. And I know that feeling – isn't going to go away. It's just going to get bigger. It's been great with you, really great, but . . . but it's time to move on. Don't you feel it?'

'Maybe. Maybe you're right. It's just – God, it's so sudden, this, it's really out of the blue for me . . .'

'I'm sorry Sean. If I'd had the guts, I'd have said something earlier.'

'You sound so *final*.'

'Oh, Sean. I'd sooner finish things between us now than let them drag on until we got so sick of each other we *hated* each other . . .'

'I don't think I'd ever hate you, Aish,' said Sean.

Aisha scrubbed at her eyes again. 'Me neither, I didn't mean that.'

There was a long silence. Sean slowly bent a beermat in two, so that it cracked along the centre. Then he sighed and said, 'You want to have like a – trial split? A break for a month or so? See how it goes?'

'Well – we could – but I think that's just something people do 'cos they can't face making the decision there and then. I mean – I don't really see the point in it.'

'No. Not if you don't fancy me any more.'

'Oh, *Sean*. Come on. Be honest. It's just not been the same, has it? For a couple of months now.'

'No. OK. It's not been the same,' said Sean dully.

'What I would like is to – is to stay friends. 'Cos that's what I think we are underneath. Don't you?'

'Yes,' he said sadly. 'Maybe you're right. I just – I thought maybe if we had a break from each other the feeling would come back.'

'I don't think it works that way,' said Aisha gently. 'If it's gone, it's gone.'

'Aisha – is there someone else?'

'No. No, Sean, there isn't. I'd have told you if there was.'

'It's just – I don't know if I could handle it if I went out tomorrow and saw you with another bloke with his arm round you.'

'Oh, look. I know. I'd feel the same. It's natural. But that's not a good enough reason to stay together, is it?' She took hold of his hand again, urgently. '*Is* it?'

Sean shook his head. 'I s'pose not,' he said.

♥

Guy Makeup

Philly was sitting in her bedroom, hugging the big old bear she'd had since she was a year old. When she heard the doorbell go and her mother's voice, answering it, complaining about how early it was, she looked up, sniffing. Then she heard footsteps pounding up the stairs and the door opened and Ian came into the room.

'Oh, *Ian*,' she said. 'Thank you – for coming over – I really wanted to . . .'

'Hello, Mopey,' he said. 'C'mere.'

He pulled the bear away from her and gathered her up to his chest, giving her a huge hug. 'Hey, what are you looking so upset for? It's Aisha and Sean who've split up, not us.'

'I *know*. But it's just so sad. I mean – they were *made* for each other.'

'No, they weren't, were they?' said Ian, pushing her hair back from her face. 'Not if this has happened.'

'I just can't *believe* it. I mean – she was going on about feeling tied down and stuff the other night, but *dumping* him . . .'

'Yeah, well. Things hadn't been right between them for ages.'

'Oh they *had*. They were great together.'

'No. They were both getting bored.'

'Have you spoken to him?'

'Yeah, last night. He called me. He's OK, honestly. He's a bit cut up and everything, but I think he knows it was the right thing . . .'

'I don't think he wanted to split up at *all*,' Philly burst out. 'I think he's just putting a brave face on it.'

'Yeah? Well, Philly-delphia, you don't know everything.'

'What don't I know?'

'Sean's been getting twitchy too. Really, he has.'

'Twitchy? Who about?'

'Just – generally.'

'When she phoned me last night, Aisha went on

and on about how they were too young to get into something heavy. She said it was stupid.' Philly looked up at Ian. 'Do *you* think it's stupid?'

'Not for us. You know I don't.'

'She went on and on about missing out on life and experience and not wanting to end up all narrow and full of regrets.'

'Blimey. Heavy. Then what did she say?'

'Oh, I don't know. Just stuff about freedom and all. She sounded all relieved and excited and – and . . .'

Ian hugged her to him again. 'Oh, come on, Philly. I mean – it must have been a relief, finally getting up the guts to tell him. And she was just trying to make herself feel she'd done the right thing.'

'So you think it's the right thing?'

'Yeah. For them.'

'And what about us?'

Ian laughed, 'Shut up, Philly. You're talking crap. You know what I feel about you.'

Then he pushed the door shut with his foot, and pulled her onto the bed with him.

* * *

The dress rehearsal was only three days away. Tasha had managed to round up Dave, Andy and Chris and drive them into the green room, so she could try out their stage makeup.

'What d'you have to try it out for?' Dave was complaining. 'Why can't you just slap it on on the night?'

'It's not that easy,' Tasha said. 'I have to play up your features so you don't get lost at the back of the stage under the lights *without* making you look like drag queens.'

'I'll go first, said Andy, settling himself into the chair and tipping his head back. 'I don't care if you make me look like a drag queen.'

'Oh, God,' muttered Dave. 'Spare us.' It was common knowledge now that Andy really fancied Tasha.

Tasha gathered up her tubes of foundation and paint, and started working on Andy's face. He kept kind of smirking as she smoothed on the makeup.

'Andy, keep a straight face,' she snapped. 'It's all going in the creases.'

'Sorry,' he breathed. 'I'll try.'

'*HI* – ya!' Karina appeared at the open door. She

seemed to know instinctively whenever Tasha had any lads in there with her. And even though Chris had been demoted to number two on her Lust List, she still wanted to keep tabs on him. Just in case it didn't work out with Aidan.

'So – how's it going, boys?' she went on. 'Getting all tarted up?'

'Just basic makeup,' said Tasha.

'Lovely! Andy – you look amazing. Hey – Tasha – am I wearing falsies for the show? False *eyelashes*, I mean,' she went on, giggling. 'It's not like I need the other sort!' And she threw her hair back and her chest out.

'Girls like you make me *ashamed* to be female sometimes,' muttered Tasha to herself, cringing. 'Yeah, I thought I'd try eyelashes on all the Pink Ladies,' she said aloud. 'I've got some here.'

'Oooh, goody. Can I see them?' squealed Karina, pushing her way into the room and squeezing past Chris far closer than she needed to. She started rummaging in the makeup box, pulling out tubes and boxes.

'Look, Karina, leave it, can't you? I've just sorted that lot out,' complained Tasha.

'Oh, ratt-*y*. I was only having a look.'

'Well, I can show you later, can't I? This place is getting pretty crowded.'

Karina turned on her heel. 'Sorry, Tasha,' she sniffed. 'Sorry if I crowded out the *room*. Sorry if I cramped your *style*.' And she swaggered out of the door.

'Jesus, that voice,' said Chris, jerking his head towards Karina's departing back. 'It goes right through your head.'

'It's like a car alarm,' added Andy. 'Drives you nuts.'

'OK,' said Tasha, giggling. 'Hold still. Eyeliner.' Carefully, she started outlining Andy's left eye with a thin black line. It was difficult to concentrate, with him breathing up at her. She was very aware of his two hands, lying tense on the arms of the chair. She had this strong instinctive feeling that they'd like to reach up and grab her.

'Wow,' said a deep voice at the door. 'Pretty boy.'

It was Aidan. He lounged in the doorway, arms folded, a sarcastic sort of a grin on his face. Tasha felt such desire when she saw him she could barely stand upright.

She managed to say 'Hi,' and smile. She felt her whole body reaching out towards him, like a plant to the sunlight, just like Andy's was reaching out to her. It's like being in some kind of sex capsule, she thought ruefully, all this lust flying about. She stooped hurriedly over Andy again, pulling his hair back from his forehead so she could work on his other eye. Andy sighed pleasurably.

'He looks too pretty,' repeated Aidan from the doorway.

'I *am* pretty,' murmured Andy. 'I'm a babe.'

'He's like – glowing,' insisted Aidan. 'Like a cornflake ad. He looks like he spends half his time working out.'

Tasha straightened up and glared at Aidan and her eyes melted into his face. 'Well, *I* can't help that,' she retorted. 'He probably *does*.'

Aidan smiled and moved into the room. 'Yeah,' he said, 'but they're supposed to be playing real hard nuts, aren't they?'

'Yeah,' admitted Tasha. 'Guys who smoke fifty a day and eat junk.'

'Well, you should make them look a bit more sick. You want to put some black round their eyes, build up some hollows under their cheekbones. Here.' And Aidan took the stick of kohl from Tasha's hand, and started to fill in shadows under Andy's eyes and around his face.

Andy was at first seriously annoyed at the switch of makeup artist. But he peered into the mirror as Aidan worked and, despite himself, he was impressed. He looked much rougher, much seedier.

'Hey,' breathed Tasha. 'That's great.'

'You want to have a go on one of the others?' asked Aidan.

Tasha took the kohl stick and started work on Chris, who bent his knees obligingly to get down to her height. Aidan watched her, standing so close that Tasha found it almost impossible to concentrate, indicating with his forefinger where she should shade in the black.

Tasha took a deep breath to give herself courage and said, 'I think you've got yourself a job, Aidan. I could do with your help on the other guys. I'm just – I'm not too good on *guy* makeup.'

Aidan laughed. 'OK. I'll drop by.' Then he turned and made for the door. Tasha let out a long sigh, hoping the three lads hadn't worked out that she'd been on the attempted pull. She thought they probably hadn't. Her pulling techniques were so subtle that usually the guy she was trying it on didn't notice, let alone anyone else.

'Weird bloke,' said Chris, when Aidan was out of earshot. 'Coming in to help with the *makeup*.'

'We should've warned him to go back the way he came,' put in Andy. 'He'll get pounced on. Karina-Hyena went that way.'

Tasha burst out laughing. 'Karina *what*?'

'Hyena. Good, eh? She's ruthless. I reckon if she wants someone, she'll go after them until they drop from exhaustion. And now it's Aidan's turn.'

'How d'you know he doesn't *want* to get pounced on?' said Tasha as casually as she could manage. 'Lots of guys find her really attractive.'

'He can't be interested. No guy could be in any doubt that he had it made with that one, the way she's been acting round him. And as far as I know, he hasn't taken up the offer.'

'Yeah, but you wouldn't know with someone like him,' said Dave, meaningfully. 'I reckon he's a real dark horse.'

♥

A Message From The Heart

Aisha was touring the shopping centre at top speed, looking for new clothes, clothes to suit the new her, telling herself that the adrenaline she was feeling was exhilaration and not sheer panic.

I've done the right thing, I've done the right thing, she repeated to herself, like a mantra. I'm free now, and it's *great*.

She'd felt nothing but exhilaration and relief yesterday evening, right after she'd talked to Sean. She felt like she'd been brave and honest and true to herself; she'd really taken control of her life, just like all the magazines told you to. Now a whole new exciting world was opening out for her, and she'd achieved this without hurting someone she really cared about, because she was sure Sean felt the same way too. They'd finished on such good terms and she was sure they could be friends now, good friends. Who says it's impossible to have it all, she'd thought, almost in triumph.

She'd gone straight home that night and phoned Philly to break the news to her. Philly had been pretty upset, too upset to be all that positive about her decision, but Aisha had expected that. It had been too late to call Tasha by the time she'd got off the phone to Philly, then she'd been all wound up and couldn't sleep properly and her night had been full of troubling, anxious dreams.

The next morning the first thing she saw when she blearily opened her eyes was Sean's picture on the ceiling, one edge peeling down towards her. She'd come to then, in a kind of confused panic, as all the events of yesterday crowded back in on her. And it suddenly felt so strange to be solo again – so weird to think she couldn't just phone Sean and chat to him.

She'd got up and dialled Philly's number instead, meaning to have another talk with her, but Philly's mum told her she'd gone out early to go swimming with Ian. 'They do all this exercise,' Philly's mum had said laughing, 'and then they blow the benefits by having a big fried breakfast afterwards.'

As Aisha put the phone down, this horrible feeling of loneliness came over her. She had a sudden clear vision of Philly and Ian sitting opposite each other in the café, hair all wet, laughing together as they dunked bread in each others' fried egg. I've got no one to do that with now, she thought. No one to just – *be* with.

Then she got dressed at top speed and headed for the shops.

Now she was standing by a rack of party dresses, picking ones at random off the rail to go and try on. They were all short, bright and sensational. It was really hard to choose between them.

In the changing room, she ripped off her jeans and pulled on one of the dresses – a purple one, with a straight, low neckline. Then she stared at her reflection in the mirror, as though she was looking at a stranger, and smiled. She pulled her long, blonde hair over to one side at the front, and tugged the hemline down a bit. 'Wow,' she said to herself. 'This looks brilliant. It'll knock their socks off at the last night party.'

She didn't bother trying any of the other dresses on. The purple one was like a talisman for the new her. She grabbed it, paid for it, then rushed out of the shop. 'I'll get some nail varnish to match,' she said to herself. But she couldn't concentrate on the shiny displays, and her hand shook as she pulled the dress out of its bag and held it up to the little bottles to compare colours.

'Aisha, what is *wrong* with you,' she muttered, walking out of the shop. 'It's OK, it's OK. I'm just jangly 'cos I need to talk to someone. I haven't really spoken to anyone since Sean and I split up. I haven't even *told* Tasha yet. Only Philly, and that was a non-starter. I need to – I need to talk it through, that's all.'

She headed for the shop exit as fast as she could, nearly colliding with a woman with a pushchair as she went out of the door. It was as though she was running away from something, as though if she moved fast enough, the feelings of doubt and panic wouldn't catch up with her again. She sped out of the shopping centre and headed for college, jumping on a bus just as the doors were folding shut.

She went straight to her locker once she got to college, meaning to lock the new dress safely away.

There, tucked into the grille at the front, was a note with 'Aisha' written on it.

Sean's writing. Unmistakable. She seized it, opened it, and read:

Aisha – please meet me at 1pm by the oak tree at the back. I've got something to tell you.
Love Sean.

Karina's Top Tips

Karina was seriously fed up. She was making no headway with Aidan at all. She'd hung around underneath his ladder trying to engage him in conversation about spotlights, and he'd answered in grunts and monosyllables and then given up answering her at all. She'd joined him at his table in the canteen, to be treated to the sight of him wolfing down his food faster than she'd thought humanly possible and then loping off, with a gruff 'See you' tossed back over his shoulder. She'd even waited for what felt like hours in the wings one night for him to finish, to make sure they left college at the same time. But all he'd done was jump on a battered looking motorbike and roar off, with not even the vaguest offer of a lift.

It was awful. It had never happened to her before

– pulling out all the stops to catch a bloke and *still* failing.

Despite not being needed for rehearsals that morning, Karina had cut classes and turned up at the drama studio, just to hang around. But Aidan had kept well out of the way, clambering around in the rafters and then disappearing under the stage, and she'd had no chance at all to get another crack at him. So now she was sitting on the edge of the stage, legs swinging, fed up.

Ness hurried by, head down. She'd just been running through her songs again and it had gone really well.

'Hey, Ness,' called out Karina. 'You sounded good then.'

Ness looked up. 'Oh . . . thanks.'

'You've really got into Rizzo's character, haven't you? Even though she's such a slag.'

Ness looked down, smiling with only one side of her mouth, and didn't reply.

'So – heard the news?' went on Karina. 'The big bust-up.'

'The big . . . ?' Ness stopped walking. She could feel her breathing quicken.

'Sean and Aisha. They've split up. She dumped him last night. Just – out of the blue. She told me this morning.' Karina had actually overheard Ian telling Charley, but she wasn't going to own up to that, eavesdropping not being as cool as sharing confidences. 'He's pretty cut up about it, apparently. What a *bitch*, dropping him right before the show.'

'Did you tell her that?'

'What?'

'That you thought she was a bitch?'

'Well – no I – *anyway*, it won't last. I mean – Aisha was going on about being restless, but it's one thing to feel restless and it's quite another to dump someone who – well, someone like Sean. Those two are *made* for each other. She'll go crawling back, begging him to take her on again.'

'You think? Aisha doesn't seem to me like the type of girl who'd crawl to anyone.'

Karina narrowed her eyes at Ness. She didn't like her attitude. Ness was supposed to be lapping this up, open mouthed, not putting in all these little niggly comments. 'Trust me,' Karina said. 'I know her. She won't last five minutes on her own. And he won't be able to resist, he's so crazy about her. And anyway – it's just *too sad* that they've split. They *have* to get back together again. Don't you think?'

'Only if they both want to,' said Ness.

Karina smiled knowingly. She'd seen Ness and Sean talking together, seen the fireworks between them on stage. Ness probably thinks she can move in now, she thought. Karina didn't like other girls thinking they could be successful with blokes, especially when she wasn't having any success herself.

'No, trust me,' she said again. 'I'll give them three days, and they'll be back in each others' arms. They split up once before, you know, and this other girl tried to move in on Sean and *boy* did she get her fingers burned! I mean – Aisha practically left her for dead! And Sean is just *besotted* with Aisha. I mean – you've only got to look at them together to see that.'

When Aisha arrived at the oak tree at one o'clock, Sean wasn't there. She stood underneath it, with her arms wrapped round herself against the cold, and waited. She could feel her throat tightening. It was their tree, the tree they met under at lunchtime in the summer to share a picnic, the tree they'd sheltered under in the rain on the way home, kissing to pass the time, standing there long after the rain had passed over. She had a sudden vision of Sean standing under it with Ness, arms about each other, and she felt like crying.

Her mind was racing, in confusion. What do I want him to say, she thought frantically, what do I want this to be about? If he comes up and begs me to get back with him, what am I going to say?

'Hey – Aisha!' Sean was walking across the grass towards her, waving. 'How're you doing?' He sounded strained.

'OK,' she said. His face looked so familiar, so warm to her. She had to stop herself throwing her arms round his neck. It was weird, the way that one conversation last night had changed everything between them, just like that.

'Anyway. Thanks for coming, Aish. And look – don't worry – I'm not going to get all heavy. It's just – it was a real bolt out of the blue, last night, and I didn't say all I wanted to, you know?'

She nodded, holding her breath.

'Actually, I've – I've got something for you.' And he drew out of his pocket a slim white box and handed it to her.

She opened it. Inside was a thin silver chain, with a tiny seahorse and two shells hanging from it. 'Oh, Sean,' she began. 'It's lovely – it's . . .'

'I bought that for our six-month anniversary,' he said. 'And last night – well, I was pretty cut up. I was looking for the receipt, thinking I'd take it back to the shop. And then I thought – no, sod it. I bought it for you for the last six months we had together, and just 'cos we've split up now, it doesn't change that. It doesn't change how good that time was, what it meant to me – what *you* meant to me.'

She looked at him, heart pounding, and suddenly with everything in her she wanted him to say 'I want you back, Aisha. Please don't do this to us.'

'Do you like it?' he said. 'Really? I know how much you love the sea. I bought it for you and – I want *you* to have it.'

She nodded, tears starting to come into her eyes. She couldn't speak.

'Look Aisha,' he went on, 'what you did last night was really – it was right. We'd got stale, you were right. It was great, together, and we had a great time, but now it's time to split, and you had the guts to say it. I see that now – now I've, you know, calmed down a bit.'

Then he smiled, and got hold of her by the elbows, like he always did, but this time when he pulled her towards him he only kissed her forehead. 'And I hope we can be friends, like you said,' he said. 'Let's give it a few weeks, eh? Get the play over with and . . . let things settle down. OK, Aish?'

She nodded, forcing herself to smile. Then he was off across the grass, leaving her.

Fast Mover

The next morning Ness was sitting alone in a corner of the canteen, hunched over a cup of cooling coffee. There was less than a week to go now before the first night. I'll be so glad when it's all over, she thought. No, I *won't*. When it's all over I won't see Sean any more. Well – I might *see* him but I won't be able to grab hold of him. I won't have an excuse to kiss him, not like now. Oh, this is such a *mess*. I'm going *mad* with it. And I wish I'd never let myself think about him splitting up with Aisha. Karina's right, he's totally hers. He's probably back together with her already.

She stared gloomily into her coffee cup, wondering whether to bother finishing it. Then, suddenly, shockingly, Sean's face was in front of her, just a few centimetres away across the table. He'd slid into the seat opposite her at the table before she was even aware he'd come into the room.

'Hi, Ness,' he said. 'Mind if I join you?'

'Bit late for that,' she croaked, hoping against hope she sounded normal, while her legs liquefied and her heart hammered. 'I seem to have been joined.'

Sean grinned. 'Can I get you another coffee or something?'

'No thanks. I was just going.'

'Don't. Stay and talk to me. How are your nerves holding up?'

'Nerves? Oh, OK I guess.'

'You're brilliant at it, you know you are. Are you thinking about going in for it – you know – professionally?'

Ness pulled a face. 'Well I'd kind of like to. But I think my mum would disown me if I did. She's always lecturing me on having a steady career.'

'Right. Accounting.'

'Banking.'

'Law.'

They both laughed, then there was a pause. 'Dress rehearsal this Monday,' said Sean.

'Yeah. I know.'

'Well I tell you, I'm freaking out at the thought of it. I mean – it's all getting a bit hyper, isn't it? D'you fancy going for a drink tonight, just to, you know, get out of here and . . .'

Ness stood up, scraping her chair backwards with a head-splitting sound. 'I can't,' she said, hoarsely. 'I – no, I can't.' Then she fled.

Sean leant his elbows on the table and let his face drop into his cupped hands. Then he swore, softly and deliberately, at the empty air.

'Well, you screwed that one up, didn't you?' said a voice behind him.

'What?' Sean looked round angrily. It was Ian standing there.

'I said you screwed that one up.'

'Where the hell did you spring from? What did you do – follow me in here?'

'Ness isn't going to go for you yet, mate. Not right after you've split up from Aisha.'

'Oh, sod off. You superior – git.'

Ian laughed and sat down beside him. 'You know – maybe it would have been better if you'd left – you know – more of a gap. Between girls.'

Sean twisted round and glared at his friend. 'She was the one that dumped me, remember? She wanted out. What does it matter to her what I do now?'

Ian shrugged. 'I wasn't thinking of Aisha, I was thinking of Ness.'

Sean collapsed again into his cupped hands. 'Oh, God, I don't know. What a mess. I mean – part of me knows Aisha's right. It was time to finish. But it's not good being dumped. It's not good at all.'

'You want to just relax, Sean.'

'Oh, shut it.'

'Ness isn't going to go away, you know. She'll keep. And you should let yourself – I dunno . . .'

'If you come out with any more touchy-feely crap, I'll . . .'

Ian laughed. 'OK. Have it your way!'

Aisha was sitting in Tasha's bedroom, hunched into a little ball on the bed. Tasha sat next to her, cradling Sean's silver chain with the seahorse and two shells on it.

'It's absolutely beautiful,' she was saying. 'To

think a *bloke* chose it. He's really something – oh, Aisha – *sorry!*'

Aisha had started weeping again. Tasha put her arm round her shoulders and cuddled her. 'Aisha, ignore me. I've got a hole in the head, seriously.'

'Don't worry,' snivelled Aisha. 'I wanted to have a good cry. That's mostly why I came to see you.'

'Good. Just so long as you didn't come for advice.'

'No. I've been avoiding Philly all day 'cos I knew she'd give me advice. Along the lines of – you have made a serious mistake. Now beg him to take you back.'

'Yeah?' Tasha reached for the tissues. 'And – *if* she said that – would you think she was right?'

'No. No, I wouldn't. Not now I've calmed down, I wouldn't. At least – I don't think I would. Oh, *God*! It's just – it hurt a lot more than I thought it was going to, Tasha. When I saw him yesterday, all I could think of was how nice he was and how good it was going around with him, how safe I felt . . .'

Tasha handed her a tissue. 'Hey, come on. Who wants to feel *safe*, Aisha? You're s'posed to be out there having a *wild time*. Wasn't that what this break-up was all about?'

Aisha smiled wanly. 'Yeah. It was. It's just – I feel so confused, somehow.'

'Course you do. You need to chill for a while and . . . calm down.'

'The thing is . . .'

'What?'

'When I saw him – I just wanted him back again.'

Tasha smiled. 'Well, I think that's natural. Ever bought something at the shops and really loved it, and then decided you hated it and were going to take it back, and then *not* taken it back after all?'

Aisha frowned. 'Yes – but what's that got to do with . . .'

'It's called buyer's remorse, right? It's a – whatsit – a *syndrome*. Well you've got – you've got finishing-with-your-boyfriend remorse. You know it's the right thing to do, you gear yourself up to do it, you do it, and then you get all the flip side coming in, all the doubts. But it was still the right thing to do just like it was a brilliant dress or whatever when you bought it. Oh, God, am I making sense? I told you I was no good at advice.'

Aisha smiled. 'No, I know what you're saying.'

'I mean – all that stuff we were talking about before – how you felt tied down and bored and stuff – that was real, wasn't it?'

'Yeah, that was real.'

'It's just that you're feeling too beat up to feel all that right now. But it'll come back. Really.'

'Yeah. You're right. It's just if I think of him with someone else . . .'

'Someone else?'

'Ness,' Aisha sniffed. 'I found myself just – spilling it all out to her. And she really likes him, I know she does. I think I thought if she got off with him, I'd be off the hook. But now . . .'

'Oh, Aisha. Stop beating yourself up.'

'Yeah. I know you're right. Hey – Tasha?'

'Mmmm?'

'What about you? How's it going with Aidan?'

'Nothing's going anywhere,' said Tasha mournfully. 'And I have never, ever had it this bad. Not ever. Not even that guy from Australia last year.'

'Yeah, well, he wasn't really all that, was he?' said Aisha, distractedly.

'Not compared to Aidan,' mooned Tasha. 'But at least he *spoke* to me. Aidan's so distant, he's so cool and . . .' she tailed off. Both the girls sighed in unison.

'Boys are the pits, aren't they?' grumbled Aisha.

'Yeah. They ruin your life. You're better off without them.'

'Yeah. Much better.'

'Hey,' said Tasha suddenly, 'why don't *we* go out tonight? Eat chocolate – see a film – it's ages since we've done that.'

Aisha smiled. 'Yeah. That's a great idea. No guys – just us. You know Tasha – you give *great* advice.'

♥

Lots Of Love Stuff

Tasha was finding life extremely difficult, because she found herself wanting to behave like Karina. She wanted to hang round Aidan's ladder, lurk in the wings hoping for a glimpse of him, accidentally-on-purpose bump into him. And being anything like Karina so horrified Tasha that it froze her up completely. She kept to her green room like a recluse, only going into the drama studio when she absolutely had to and then keeping her head down and rushing out again.

She thought about Aidan all the time, though. And this was more than was healthy, she told herself. She thought about his voice, and his face, and the way he half-grinned when he looked at her, and she especially thought about the way his shoulders tensed when he lifted his heavy equipment.

There was no doubt about it. She had it bad.

'You carry on at this rate,' she said to herself severely, 'and you are going to be completely hysterical when he shows up to help with the makeup at the dress rehearsal. IF he shows up.' She'd fixed on that as her big chance – although when she actually thought about trying to move in on him with Dave, Chris and Andy in the room – and Andy still trying to move in on her – she was filled with despair. I can't do it, she thought. Not with that lot there. Not doing their makeup. No one could. Not even Karina.

The technical rehearsal was being held that afternoon. Tasha turned up at the drama studio at two o'clock sharp with a list and a red pen and found herself a seat at the side. Most of the responsibility for the costume changes rested on her and she felt pretty daunted by it.

You could practically reach out and touch the tension in the studio. This was *it* – if this went badly, it didn't auger well for the dress rehearsal. Everyone was talking too loudly and laughing too much, and Bill was stamping around, bossily yelling orders and encouragement.

'OK,' Bill shouted finally. 'I want a clean run through. We'll take it just like the full dress rehearsal – but without the clothes.'

'Get 'em off!' Charley shouted.

'Yes, ha, ha,' said Bill. 'You know what I mean. Now let's GO!'

For the first hour, Tasha concentrated furiously, timing scenes and writing notes in urgent red. Then out of the corner of her eye, she saw Aidan lope across the studio and into the wings. Two minutes later, he crossed back again. She felt her whole self leaning out towards him once more, magnetised by him. 'Concentrate,' she muttered, staring down hard at her list. 'Ignore all distractions.'

But Aidan was a big distraction. He lounged against the wall opposite her, head on one side as he checked the position of the spotlights falling on the stage, then he crossed back again and disappeared into the wings. Tasha sighed and scribbled three large asterisks at random on her list.

On the stage, the boys were into one of their all-singing, all-dancing numbers. Tasha tried to focus on them. The routine had retained an exciting feeling that at any minute all seven would crash into each other.

Suddenly a low voice at her side said, 'It's crap, isn't it?' and Aidan slithered down to a sitting position right next to her.

'What?' Tasha croaked. She felt as if she might hyperventilate with delight – and shock. Why did he go in for such *sudden* appearances?

'It's all crap,' he said. 'The music and the dancing – it's so *dated*.'

'It's meant to be dated,' said Tasha. 'It's set in the fifties.'

There was a pause during which Tasha slid her eyes sideways to look at Aidan and then had to look away again quickly, because if her heart went any faster she thought she'd pass out. He was so close, she only had to lean a little to her left and she'd be touching him.

'I used to dance,' Aidan announced.

'Yeah?'

'Semi-professional.'

'Really? D'you still do it?'

'Nah. It took up too much time – and the ego with dancers, it's all as bad as that lot up there.

Worse.' He grinned. 'I could show them a thing or two, bet they'd've loved me muscling in, wouldn't they. I mean – they'd really appreciate me pointing out to them what crap movers they are.'

Tasha laughed. Aidan turned to look at her. 'That one I put the stage makeup on – Andy is it? He's got the hots for you like – like anything. You noticed?'

Tasha could feel herself going bright, bright red with pleasure. When guys started talking to you about who fancied you it was always, in her experience, a good sign. It meant they might fancy you too. 'Yes. I noticed,' she said. 'How come *you* noticed?'

'How? Have to have your head in a sack not to. He was watching you the whole time I was in your room. You'd better be careful with that one, girl.'

'Yeah? Well – you'd better watch out for Karina.'

'Oh, her – she *scares* me. Lucky for me she always makes so much noise I know she's coming and get time to scarper.'

Tasha laughed, and inside she was crowing. Oh, Karina, too *bad*, she thought.

Up on the stage, the cast had reached the interval. Bill gathered them all around him while he commented on their performances. 'It went OK, I think,' whispered Tasha.

'No major balls-ups then?'

'None that I could see.'

'Yeah. They all look pretty smug, don't they. I guess they'll all be really happy with themselves when they're through. Lots of luvvie kissing, yeah?' And he leant towards her and made a mocking *mwaah mwaah* kiss to each side of her face.

Tasha felt delicious shock waves, even if he hadn't actually made contact with her skin. It was incredible, that breaking of the space boundary between them, just incredible. Aidan didn't draw away from her immediately either – and for one ecstatic moment she thought he was going to end up in the centre and kiss her on the mouth.

But he didn't. He moved back, although not as far as he'd been before. 'You're a real sod,' she said, giggling. 'They're not that bad. I haven't seen a single one of them give a kiss like that *ever*.'

'No – just the other sort, eh?' On the stage, Sean had turned to talk to Ness, who had edged away from him, head lowered, and now Philly had her hand gripped on Sean's arm, holding him back, saying something to him, very intently. Aisha stood to one side, watching them all in silence. Then Bill called for the second half to start.

'Whooo,' muttered Aidan. 'Lots of love stuff there.'

'Yes, there is,' agreed Tasha. 'But what are you, psychic?'

'No. Just a top-grade eavesdropper.' He turned to grin at her, and she managed to meet his eyes. There was so much electricity between them now you could run a generator off it. 'Hey – I'd better go,' he said. 'I'm supposed to be adjusting the spots on Joel, this scene. He wants them brighter. Maybe if I push the volts up I can white him out all together, eh? Bye!'

Tasha laughed and said 'Bye,' as he scrambled to his feet, then she wrapped her hands round her knees and hugged herself as tightly as she could bear. She felt as if she might shoot up to the ceiling in sheer excitement if she didn't. 'That was *fab – u – lous*,' she said to herself.

♥

Aisha Works Out

As soon as the technical rehearsal was over, Ness fled. Sean had tried to talk to her again, then Philly had glared at her and said something very intense to Sean and all the time Aisha was standing at the back all alone and forlorn and silent – it was all absolutely *horrible*.

'No way,' she muttered to herself, '*no* way. I'm not getting caught up in all that. And if Karina's right – I'll be the one that gets hurt. They'll all think I'm a right bitch. I don't care how gorgeous Sean is, I'm not getting involved.'

The next morning, Aisha borrowed her older brother's mountain bike, put on two jumpers and some scratchy woollen gloves, and headed for the woods by the college sports centre. There was a mist in the air and frost on the grass by the roadside, and flurries of tiny birds, stripping the bushes of the last of the berries, flew up as she passed. Aisha laughed with exhilaration as she speeded up a gear. 'It's fine, being on my own,' she said to herself. 'It's more than fine, it's *great*.'

Sitting around moping, she decided, was no way to sort herself out. She was going to get physical. It was harder going in the woods, but Aisha was determined. Crouching low over the handlebars she raced along, her lungs aching from the cold air, and soon she skidded to the end of the lane and rode out onto the huge playing fields.

In the distance by the sports centre building was the running track, with four figures, all spaced out, circling it. As Aisha freewheeled towards it she focused on the tallest of them. It was Dave, she was sure of it, with his broad shoulders and dark hair spiked back in the wind. She felt a pulse of excitement as she stopped by the edge and waited.

Dave circled the track towards her, then slowed for a stride or two and waved. 'Hey – Aisha! What're you doing here?'

'I've come to check out the gym,' she called back. 'See what classes are on offer.'

'I've got two more laps to do – then I'll show you round!' he shouted, then he pounded past her and raced off round the track once more.

Aisha sat back on her bike seat, smiling wryly. God forbid that you cut your training session short for *me*, she thought. She watched as he lengthened his stride, intent on impressing her. Then he was jogging up to meet her, sweaty, gorgeous and grinning. 'So,' he said, 'decided to get fit, have you? Or should I say – fit*ter*?'

He's been working on that for the last five minutes, Aisha thought. 'Well,' she replied, smiling, 'I just thought I should sign up for something. I mean – I do two dance classes a week, but I just don't feel it's enough.'

'Well – three times a week of extended aerobic activity's generally thought to be . . .' and he was off on some technical lecture about balancing fitness levels with upper-body strength. Together they wandered along the edge of the track and up to the sports centre building. Dave showed her where to lock up her bike, and then she followed him inside.

'You look cold,' he said. 'The end of your nose is all red.'

'Well, thanks,' she said sarcastically. 'And actually, I'm freezing.'

'Fancy some hot chocolate?'

'Oh, yeah. Please.'

Dave marched over to a drinks machine standing in the corner, fed in some money, pressed some buttons, them presented Aisha with a little plastic cup of steaming chocolate. Then he punched the buttons for some 'super-isotonic fluid replacement', with pictures of manic athletes all over the can, for himself.

'Come on,' he said. 'I'll show you the gym. I usually do a half-hour workout there after I've been running.'

As they entered the gym, Aisha found herself getting the giggles. 'Aisha, what are you *doing* here,' she muttered to herself, as she stalked self-consciously past a huge guy lifting barbells. 'Dave might be seriously gorgeous, but this isn't exactly your scene is it? Jesus, I'm the only girl here.'

Dave had started to show her the weights, running through his own routine stage by stage as though every detail of it was deeply fascinating. Then he made her sit down at a huge machine, like an upright modern version of the rack, and heave some weights up and down herself. I feel like a complete prat, Aisha thought, as she pulled on the bar. I *am* a complete prat.

'Not bad,' Dave said. 'D'you want me to work you out a routine? You need to do it at least three times a week, and each time you do it, you increase the repetitions by five, and gradually you increase the weights, just by a little each time, say a kilogram or two, and . . .'

In desperation, Aisha looked at her watch and let out a shriek. 'I should've been gone ten minutes ago! Sorry . . . meeting Tasha . . . She'll kill me if I'm late.'

'Well, that's a pity,' said Dave. 'I was going to suggest you hung about while I did my workout and then I could show you the sauna.' And he laid a large hand suggestively on her arm.

Aisha felt something close to panic. 'Sorry,' she said. 'Gotta go! Maybe I'll turn up again, come running with you, eh?'

'Er, OK,' Dave said, confused. 'See you later.

And then maybe we can work you out a programme.'

'Er – right. OK, then, bye. See you at the dress rehearsal.' Then she fled, jumped on her bike, and raced over the wide spaces of the playing fields.

Avoidance Tactics

The day of the dress rehearsal arrived. Tasha was barricaded into the green room with costumes ranged around her, feeling like she was in a war zone. Aidan was adrift somewhere up in the rafters, trying to sort out a flickering problem, and the whole cast were high as kites and loud as sirens.

But when it finally got started the rehearsal went well, almost without a hitch. Joel stumbled against Chris in one of the dance scenes but Chris managed to bounce him back on his feet with style. Karina muffed up some of her lines but covered it with a high-pitched squeal of laughter quite in character for Marty. Everything else was fine. Bill mopped his brow at the finish, congratulated the whole cast, then told them to get changed, clear off and rest. 'I want tomorrow night's performance to be even more *terrific* than this,' he said. 'The tickets are *sold out*!'

Everyone went off to get changed. Sean cleaned up fast and left the boys' room just in time to see Ness disappearing out of a side door, carrying the old record-player from the sleepover scene. Quickly, he followed her. She skirted the dark corridor behind the stage then disappeared into the props room. Sean walked straight over and went in too.

Ness spun round from the shelves to face him. 'Sean!' she said, shakily, 'what do you want?'

Sean took in a breath. 'I'll tell you what I want,' he said. 'I want you to stop avoiding me.'

'What do you mean?'

'Ness, I just want you to talk to me.'

'I've *been* talking to you.'

'No – you *used* to talk to me, but now you don't. Now you don't say more than two sentences to me. And you head in the opposite direction every time I appear. Why?'

Ness looked down, refusing to answer. He moved towards her. 'What's the matter?' he demanded. 'We used to get on fine.'

'I know . . . I know,' Ness said, flustered. 'But – look – I don't want to get into any complicated stuff, OK? I've seen the way Aisha looks at me. I don't think your girlfriend likes how well we get on together.'

'*Ness*! Don't pretend you don't know. Everyone knows. Aisha isn't my girlfriend now. We split up.'

Ness looked down at the floor and shrugged. 'Yeah, but for how long?'

'What d'you mean, for how long? We're finished. That's why I asked you out for that drink.'

'Well, I don't fancy getting caught up in a collision course when you get back together again.'

'What *are* you on about? We're not getting back together again. I told you – it's over.'

'Like it was last time?'

'*What*? We've never split up before.'

'But Karina said . . .'

'*Karina*? Since when has anyone listened to what old motormouth has to say? What's she been saying, anyway?'

Ness half-smiled. 'I thought you didn't listen to her. She said . . . she said how you and Aisha had split up once before, then got back together again, because you were both so crazy about each other and so right for each other.'

'Well, she made that up. We've never even had a little split over a row or something. And Ness – we're *not* crazy about each other. Not any more. It's over, honestly.'

There was a long stretch of silence. Sean moved across the room and sat down on a pile of folded, old, red curtains. 'Jesus, these are filthy,' he said, batting at the clouds of dust that rose up. 'Ness, now you know the truth – you going to talk to me again? What're you so nervous about?'

Ness turned away, moved in a semicircle round the room, then came to a standstill in front of Sean, staring down at him. She looked as though she'd made up her mind about something.

'Sean – I'm new here,' she said.

'Well, you don't say. I thought you'd been here for years. I thought you'd . . .'

'I'm serious. What I mean is – it's not easy being new. And I really like Aisha and Philly and . . . I don't want to screw things up by – by . . .'

'By going out with me?'

'Look, I know you just asked me out for a *drink*. I'm not saying you and I are *involved* or anything, it's just . . .'

'Just that we could be,' interrupted Sean, 'and you know it.'

Ness looked down at the ground, heart beating fast. What she'd most wanted to happen was happening, and she wasn't sure she could cope with it. 'Oh, God,' she said. 'I just – I mean – Aisha's been looking *so* upset . . .'

'Aisha and I are over,' Sean said seriously. 'Really over. So you wouldn't be screwing anything up. No one could blame you for anything.'

Ness's heart was pounding. She smiled down at Sean. 'Is that another invitation?' she asked.

He got to his feet. 'Yes,' he said. 'Yes, if you want it to be.'

Ness slowly put out her hand and laid it on Sean's arm, and he covered it with his hand, and then they leant towards each other.

'Yes please,' said Ness. Sean laughed and wound his arms around her. Then – as though they didn't have a choice – they were kissing.

♥

First Night Nerves

Fifteen minutes later, Ness and Sean were still wrapped around each other in the props room. Moving apart was out of the question.

'All right?' asked Sean, as he gently tucked some of her hair behind her ear.

'Yeah,' she breathed, 'definitely.' She still couldn't believe it had happened, that she was kissing him for real, at last. She moved her hands slowly up his arms, then she wound her arms round his neck. He grinned, and bent to kiss her once more.

'Ness,' said Sean after a while, 'this is just – this is so – I've wanted to kiss you properly ever since the first rehearsal. It just about finished me off, you know, when we had to *act* kissing?'

'Yeah, me too,' said Ness. 'I felt like that.'

'Yeah? And all the time we were dancing together

and holding each other – I kept thinking I'd get carried away and you'd whack me one.'

Ness laughed. 'I'm not sure I would've whacked you. I found it pretty hard myself.'

'It was so hot between us on stage, right? And everyone thought we were great actors, but really . . .'

'. . . we just really fancied each other!'

'Yeah. No one's acting's *that* good.'

'No. Well. And I was – I was – oh, you'll think I'm silly.'

'What?' said Sean, grinning.

'I used to think I'd never have the nerve to grab you like Rizzo grabs Kenickie.'

Sean laughed. 'Proved yourself wrong, then?'

'Yep. Definitely.' And she reached up and pulled his head down to hers and proved it all over again.

'Oh, Ness,' Sean sighed, hugging her in really close to him, 'you're fantastic. I thought so the first time I saw you. And then when we got on so well and had such a laugh . . .'

'Yeah. It was too much.'

'Not any more.'

'No. But I don't think we should like – rub Aisha's nose in it, do you?'

'She dumped me, you know. I was the wounded party.'

'Yeah, yeah. But I mean – I really like her and this is so soon. And there's such a thing as *tact*, you know, and . . .'

Sean laid a finger on her lips. 'I can keep a secret if you can,' he said.

First night. First night. No matter how many first nights you've had, you never really get used to swapping the empty, echoing space of the rehearsal hall for the packed, breathing, heaving lines of the audience. Philly held the curtain up a fraction and peered anxiously out. 'It's like some great *animal* out there,' she whispered, dramatically.

'Well, let's just hope it's friendly,' Ian muttered, then he put his arm round her shoulders and squeezed reassuringly.

Eight o'clock. Right on cue, the music started up. Joel dropped his prima donna first-night-nerves mode and burst on to the stage like a professional. Within ten minutes they had the audience right with them. Lots of laughter, and clapping and catcalls after the musical numbers.

The interval arrived in a heartbeat and Bill gathered all the actors round him like some kind of manic football manager. 'OK, kids, it's going *brilliantly*,' he said. 'Just don't let it go off the boil, OK? Don't get complacent. Keep that *energy* up front. Ness and Sean – what happened to *you*? It was *magic*.'

Charley mimed throwing up and Sean looked down, grinning, not daring to meet Ness's eye. Then they were off on the second half.

The final applause was deafening. 'I know what they mean now when they say it brought the house down,' said Charley triumphantly, as they all finally staggered off the stage. 'I really thought the ceiling was gonna come in.'

'That was just ... mind blowing,' breathed Philly.

'We did it, we really *did* it,' chanted Ness ecstatically.

'That was brilliant,' gloated Aisha. 'That was

such a *buzz*.' And she threw her arms round Ness and hugged her.

As they clattered off to the changing rooms, Tasha was gathering up all the costumes a bit grumpily. She was very happy that the show had gone so spectacularly well, but she was also just a little fed up at being treated like an invisible housemaid. As she scurried back and forth picking up after everyone, checking for stains and tears, hardly anyone said a word to her. They were still all too full of what had happened on stage.

Well, she could get over that, but she couldn't get over the fact that her plan to get off with Aidan had flopped, just as she'd feared. He'd turned up to help with the makeup like he'd promised, but it had been like trying to get off with someone when you're working side-by-side on a top-speed production line. There was no time for conversation – there was no time to even *look* at each other. The only words he said to her were, 'Got another kohl stick?' To which she replied 'Yeah.' Then, as soon as he'd done the three lads, he was gone, because Bill was shouting about one of the footlights failing.

'Oh, *sod* it,' she muttered, almost in tears, as she

stomped back to the green room. 'I can't *bear* it. It's like trying to make contact with – with *Venus*, he's so out of reach.' She dumped a pile of clothes on the sofa, and miserably began to hook them onto hangers, one by one. 'I've got to make sure he comes to the last-night party,' she muttered. 'It's my last chance before he disappears and I never see him again!'

Sean had his jacket on ready to go. He left the boys' changing room and wandered along the corridor, hands in pockets. Ness was standing there chatting with Aisha and Philly and some of the girls from the chorus, all of them still happily mulling over the evening's success.

'Night, girls,' Sean called out. 'Get some jaw rest before tomorrow.' He laughed at the insults that followed this and walked past them, letting his shoulder knock against Ness's as he did.

Ness looked at his retreating rear view and smiled to herself. Then a few seconds later she announced to the group that she'd better be going or she'd miss the last bus, and followed after him.

The door of the prop room had been left ajar. Ness slid round it into the dark and immediately a pair of arms enfolded her. Then Sean was covering her face in kisses.

'What's the matter?' she laughed. 'Didn't you get enough of me on stage?'

'No,' he said, 'and it's the greasepaint. I can't stand the taste of it.'

She buried her face in his neck, greedily inhaling the scent of his hair, his skin. 'Did you feel weird tonight?' she said. 'Different?'

'It felt great. This feels better.'

'D'you think anyone spotted we weren't acting any more?'

'Nah. They just think we're up for an Oscar.'

'Especially Bill. He's such an idiot, that guy.'

'Don't you knock Bill. I love the man.'

'Yeah?'

'Yeah. He put you in the show didn't he?'

Ness laughed and wrapped her arms tighter round Sean's chest.

♥

Last Night Lust

The second night of the show went off with the same noisy success as the first and hardly a hitch. Then the last night arrived. The atmosphere in the auditorium from the outset was electric, on stage and off. Joel was going into mega-star mode because his actor dad had turned up with several of his cronies.

'This could be my *big* break,' Joel squawked. 'Derek Baskerville's out there, and he's *huge*, he's like this *huge* director, he makes these *enormous* films . . .'

'. . . and if you weren't such a *gigantic* prat,' interrupted Ian, 'he might give you a part in one, right?'

'My cue,' snapped Joel, and stalked onto the stage, sticking his chin in the air.

Tucked into a quiet corner behind the scenes, Sean had got hold of Ness again. 'What happened to "I can keep a secret if you can?"' Ness teased.

'OK, OK,' said Sean. 'Just one kiss.'

Minutes later, Charley brushed past them. 'Lay off, we're on next,' he said. 'You'll be done on an obscenity charge.'

Sean laughed. 'He's right. OK, back off Ness, you animal.'

'HAH! Me, an animal?' Ness laughed and she prised herself reluctantly away from him.

When the show finished and the encores were over, Bill strode to the front of the stage. 'I don't want to make a long speech . . .' he began. It was hard to hear what he was saying above the cacophony, but his grin told the full story of the show. Philly had remembered to do a quick whip round for him and they'd bought him a bottle of scotch for all his hard work, which Aisha duly presented with a kiss.

'Oh, and one last thing,' bellowed Bill, 'before you all go. As I'm sure you all realise, a lot of work goes on backstage to produce a show like this. And I have two special thanks to give –

to Tasha, our wonderful makeup and costume girl, and to Aidan, who did such a ... er ... such an *innovative* job with the lights. Come on out, you two!' And he flung out both arms, hopefully.

In the wings, Tasha was cringing. 'Oh, God, *no*,' she muttered. She didn't move.

'Get *on* there,' shrieked Aisha, pushing her forwards.

Half pleased, half appalled, Tasha slouched onto the stage. 'OK, here's the lady we owe the look of this thing to – now where's the guy who lit it up?' called Bill.

There was a pause. The stamping in the hall increased. Finally Aidan appeared at the back of the stage.

Over the catcalls, he walked to the front, and grinning, held out his hand to Tasha. She found her hand reaching straight out to take it, then they faced the front and bowed together.

Then the whole cast came back on stage and, in the hubbub, Tasha looked down at her hand, still beautifully enclosed in Aidan's. She wondered if she was supposed to pull it away. She didn't want to. 'All right,' she said urgently to herself. 'You won't get a better chance than this. Now *go for it.*'

'Are you coming to the cast party?' she croaked.

'What cast party?' Aidan asked.

'Oh, *Aidan*. Don't tell me you haven't heard about it!'

'Well – I guess.' He looked at her, and somehow their hands drifted apart.

'Oh – come on. It'll be a laugh. It's in the back room at the *Turks' Head*. You know it? It's only five minutes' walk, it's . . .'

'Yeah, I know it. Look – I'll try,' he said, walking off backstage again.

Aisha had laid her pre-party preparation plans with extreme care. No turning up with black all round the eyes and blobs of cold cream in the hair for *her*. And no schlepping along in stage costume either – Sandy's gear was too naff for words. No, Aisha had it sorted. She had full skincare and makeup kit and the new purple dress she'd bought stashed away in her bag, and now she sought a quiet corner in the girls' toilets to put it all on. And if she was a bit late to the party, so be it. Late entrances were dramatic, right?

Back in the girls' changing room, Ness, Philly and Karina were on a real high. Ness looked in the mirror, wiped off the top layer of her red lipstick and shrugged. 'C'mon, let's go,' she said, turning to the others. 'I can't be bothered to get all this off. I hereby promise myself a face-pack at the weekend to make amends.'

'Yeah,' said Philly. 'Let's just get there.'

'*Yeah*,' squealed Karina. 'And when we get there – stay in character. Let's behave like total tarts all night.'

Resisting the impulse to say so *what would be different for you Karina*? Ness laughed and asked, 'Anyone seen Aisha?'

Philly shrugged. 'Dunno where she is. And I said I'd give Tasha a shout. We were all going to go down there together.'

'Tasha's in the green room still,' said Karina. 'I'll get her. She gets really pissed off if I don't drop in on her, you know. You find Aisha.' And she left.

In the green room, Tasha was in a flap. Whatever interpretation she tried to weld on to them, Aidan's last words had not been encouraging. *I'll try*. Not exactly the passionate avowal of someone keen to get to grips with me, she thought. What happened to that connection they'd made, the day of the technical rehearsal? Had she dreamt it or something?

But just in case he *did* turn up – she needed to look a whole lot better than she did right now. She wanted a shower for a start. She tried telling herself that being hot and sweaty was earthy and animalistic, but didn't quite believe it herself.

'*Tash*-a!' screeched Karina, jamming her head round the door. 'What are you *doing* in here? Time to go!'

'Oh, God, look at me,' Tasha groaned, peering into the mirror. 'I look like an undercooked chip. Look at my *hair*.'

Karina came and stood behind her and looked into the glass. 'Yeah, I see what you mean,' she said helpfully. 'Never mind. No one's going to notice it's gone all flat.' Then she turned and sashayed out of the room, calling back, 'Anyway, look at *me*! I'm going along in full stage makeup!'

Yeah, thought Tasha sourly, as she followed her, and it doesn't look that different from your normal stuff. If anything, it's more *subtle*.

Party On

'So – anyone asked Aidan along?' asked Philly, glancing at Tasha.

'Yeah,' said Karina. 'I did.'

'And?'

'He didn't sound keen.'

Philly rolled her eyes at Tasha as they pushed open the door to the pub. 'He'll turn up,' she whispered.

'No he won't,' replied Tasha dolefully.

They hadn't found Aisha anywhere, and in the end Tasha, Ness, Karina and Philly had made their way to the party without her. They knew all the lads would be already there, clearing off the food table as fast as possible.

Ness saw Sean as soon as they walked in, but she stopped short of going over and claiming him as hers. There was a great post-show feeling between her and Tasha and Philly now and she didn't want to wreck it. She waited until Ian had jumped on Philly, and Karina was noisily pirouetting round the sporty lads, then she sidled up to Sean and said, 'Alright?'

Sean smiled. 'Yeah,' he said, as he got hold of her hand behind her back and squeezed it, running his fingers over hers.

Tasha stood to the side of the room and watched the door. Even when she turned her back on it, she felt she was watching it, willing it to open and let Aidan come in. It was opening less and less frequently now. Just about everyone had got to the party and the noise level was incredible. She could feel a kind of weight inside her, getting heavier as the minutes ticked by.

'Hey,' said Philly, appearing at her side, 'let's get our plates stacked up. Before the table is cleared completely.'

'I don't feel hungry,' said Tasha.

'Oh, come on, Tasha. Eat something.' Philly grabbed her by the arm and dragged her over to the food table. Now that the first explosion of excitement was over, everyone realised how starved they were and sausages, pizza, bhajis and samosas were disappearing fast. Even the strips of raw vegetables round the dips were looking encroached on.

'Aisha's not here yet, is she,' said Philly, mouth full.

'No,' said Tasha. 'I just hope she doesn't get too upset when she does get here.' And she motioned over to Sean and Ness, on the far side of the table. Their eyes were glued on each other and the magnetism between them was practically visible.

'So are they really an item now?' asked Philly.

'Yeah. I'm sure they are. They're just being . . . tactful.'

'Aw, bless,' said Philly.

Charley materialised between them. 'They weren't being tactful in the wings tonight,' he said.

'Yeah, well,' said Philly. 'Ian said Sean's fancied her for ages.'

'I'll say he has,' said Charley. He turned to Tasha. 'So, costume queen! You finally got public recognition.'

'Yup.'

'A curtain call with the lighting dude. Is he coming tonight?'

Tasha shrugged. 'Dunno.'

'You don't fool me,' Charley laughed. 'You've been watching that door like a hawk.'

'I have not!'

'Yeah you have. The woman who wouldn't melt ice cubes in her mouth has finally got the hots for someone.'

'Oh, sod off, Charley,' snapped Tasha. 'You don't know what you're talking about.'

'Don't I?' he smirked and wandered off.

'Gobby little git,' she muttered to herself. 'Who's he think he is?'

Then Andy pitched up, making soulful eyes at her. 'Any food left?' he said.

'We haven't had seconds yet,' said Chris.

'Poor *things*,' said Tasha, sarcastically. 'Yeah – a bit.'

'Also – I needed to escape,' said Chris. 'Karina was moving in on me.'

'Like a tank,' added Andy.

'Protect me, Tasha,' said Chris, plaintively.

'Get lost,' laughed Tasha, and the three of them turned to the food table again. Just as they were scooping up the last of the dip, a blast of music filled the room. 'Here we go,' groaned Tasha. 'Bill's turned the sound system up.'

Almost immediately, Bill burst on to the floor, doing a kind of insane, seventies, arm-waving boogie. Karina, screaming with laughter, joined him. 'Oh, sod it,' Tasha said to herself. 'He's not coming!' She took a deep breath. Then she grabbed Andy's and Chris's hands. 'Come on,' she said. 'Let's fill up the floor.'

One of the things that Tasha did really well, and knew she did really well, was dance. When she moved, she responded to every level of the music, fluid and easy. Andy went into turbo-drive beside her, while Chris kept both of them between him and Karina.

Two records later, the door opened once more. Tasha looked up. She felt as though her heart was halfway up her throat, choking her.

But it was Aisha. And Aisha was looking fabulous, with her new dress and her hair long and loose. All the girls in their stage makeup suddenly looked a bit clownish beside her.

'Hey!' yelled Joel, heading over. 'It's my leading lady!'

Dave didn't waste a second either – he was at her side immediately. 'You never made it back to the gym,' he said.

'No – well,' said Aisha. 'I was kind of afraid of straining something.' Like my boredom threshold, she thought.

'You want something to eat?' Joel persevered.

Aisha glanced over at the devastated food table. 'I think I'm a bit late for that. Want to dance?'

'Yeah, great!' said Dave and Joel simultaneously, starting to move.

'Look at Aisha,' said Ness, glancing sideways up at Sean's face, trying to read his expression. '*Two* guys after her. You jealous?'

Sean looked down at Ness, grinning. 'What have *I* got to be jealous about?' he said. 'Come on – let's crowd the floor out some more.'

Within fifteen minutes, the dance floor was packed, everyone heaving and jiving. Bill's wife had moved onto the floor too and was now practically wrestling with him, trying to persuade him it was time to leave. And then the door to the pub backroom swung open yet again and Aidan walked in.

♥

Curtain Down

Aidan stood in the doorway, looking around at everyone. And Tasha knew, ecstatically, looking across the room at him, she knew, without a shadow of a doubt, that he really didn't want to be here at all and the only reason he'd turned up – was because of *her*. She left the crowded floor and headed over to the doorway. She felt full of confidence, bursting with it.

'Hi,' she said.

'Hi,' Aidan replied.

There was a pause, then Tasha grinned. 'You made it then,' she said.

He shrugged. 'Yeah.'

Tasha looked at his face, and she felt as though her legs might fold under her with sheer pleasure. 'You've been ages,' she said.

'Well – I had to lug about fifty light attachments below stage, all by myself.'

'Poor *thing*! No one to help you?'

'No.'

'All the food's gone.'

He smiled. 'I don't care.'

'So you too tired to dance, now?' Tasha said. 'Come on – you said you were a dancer.'

Grinning, Aidan took her hand for the second time that night and they moved onto the floor together. And Aidan proved he could dance. Nothing showy, nothing too energetic – just there with the rhythm, moving with it, at one with it. Tasha was the perfect partner for him. She could feel all eyes on her, feel the amazement and envy from half the girls in the room, and that and the sheer bliss she felt sharpened her performance. She and Aidan prowled round each other, always the same distance apart, as though they were joined by a thread you couldn't see.

Then her pleasure was cut short. Karina sprang across the floor, shrieking 'Ai-*dan*! I thought you weren't com-*ing*!'

Aidan looked at Tasha, his eyes begging – *bail*

me out! Then he turned to Karina. 'Well – I – I kind of made a date,' he said.

'Yeah,' said Tasha, stepping forward and linking her arm through his, 'with me. OK, Karina?'

Karina looked like she'd been slapped round the face. 'O-*K*,' she said, nastily. 'Don't *worry* – I can take a hint.'

'That must be a first – Karina taking a hint,' muttered Aidan, as she flounced off across the floor.

'Oh, don't,' murmured Tasha. 'You could almost feel sorry for her. Almost.'

'So. On our next date . . .'

'Our next date?' she breathed, hardly daring to believe her ears.

'Well, this *is* a date – we just agreed it was.'

Tasha smiled up at him. 'OK. On our next date . . . ?'

'Can we go somewhere where there aren't any actors?'

'Sure,' laughed Tasha, then they started dancing again, even closer than before.

The lights got lower, the music got slower, the

doors to the little terrace outside were flung open despite the cold, and couples started wandering out there for some privacy.

Aisha had managed to dump Joel by the not-so-subtle method of dancing so close to Dave that there wasn't a hair's breadth between them. Then, Joel gone, she'd spun round to include Chris and Andy, who was looking a bit bereft since Tasha's departure, and then other people joined them, and soon they were all dancing about in a big, noisy group. She felt great, dancing and flirting, joking and laughing.

Philly careered across the floor, towing Ian behind her. 'Aisha, you look fantastic,' she said. 'That dress is just *brilliant*! When can I borrow it?'

'Never,' laughed Aisha, turning to dance opposite her. 'Hey – have you seen who Tasha's with?'

'Yes – thank God – isn't it great? And are you – are you . . . ?'

'I'm having a *ball*,' said Aisha, happily spinning away again.

At the first really slow number, Aidan and Tasha faltered, stopped dancing, looked at each other, then Aidan stepped forward and Tasha did too.

Then in one amazing movement their arms were round each other. Tasha sighed with sheer pleasure and rested her face on his chest. She closed her eyes and greedily breathed him in.

'Glad you came?' she whispered, as they started to sway together, and his hands moved slowly up her back, onto her shoulders . . .

'You bet,' he said.

'Even though it's full of egos?'

'I'm not really noticing the egos any more,' he said, then he pulled her in close and bent down to kiss her, slowly, sure of himself, and Tasha kissed him back.

Sean came back from the bar, a drink in each hand. He grinned wickedly at Ness. 'C'mere!' he said.

Ness smiled, took both drinks from Sean and put them down on a side table. Then Sean slid his hands slowly round her waist and pulled her towards him.

For the next hour, Ness and Sean, and Tasha and Aidan were not really conscious of anyone else but the person right in front of them. And all Aisha was conscious of was dancing her feet off and having the most fun she'd had in months.

Then Tasha and Aisha collided together in the Ladies. '*Alright, Tasha,*' crowed Aisha. 'You did it!'

Tasha laughed happily. 'He is – he's amazing, Aisha.'

'Yeah, yeah. I know. I can *see*. Well, you did it Tasha. You held out for the one you really wanted and you got him!'

'I still can't believe it.'

'You'd better. He's out there waiting for you. I saw him when I came in.'

Tasha gave a sort of shudder of pleasure and got her hairbrush out of her bag.

'So,' Aisha went on. 'What's he like, then?'

'Oh – *Aisha!*'

Aisha grinned at her. 'S'OK. I can tell just by looking at you. You jammy cow.'

'Yeah – anyway – what about Dave?'

'What about him? All biceps and no brain.'

Both girls shrieked with laughter. Then they leaned towards the mirror, checking their reflections. 'Oh, Aisha,' said Tasha. 'Are you really OK?'

'Yes,' said Aisha, firmly. 'I feel . . . I feel better

about myself than I have done for ages. I'm just having fun, Tasha.'

'And do you mind about . . .'

'Sean and Ness? No, I don't. I really don't. It's a bit weird, but they were so sweet when I got here – not being really blatant about it. And there was me having a complete ball. I mean – it feels great, being a free agent, Tasha, it really does. Having some space.'

'Yeah?' said Tasha dreamily. 'Lend us your lippy.'

'Here. Yeah, it does. I mean – I know you can't imagine it at the moment. Jesus, you can hardly *focus* at the moment. But it does.'

The girls left the loo and ran straight into Philly and Ian talking to Sean and Ness. Philly was waving her arms about excitedly. 'I *swear* it,' she was saying. 'Come on – I'll show you!'

'What's up?' asked Aisha.

'Follow us,' said Ian, 'and you'll find out.' Aisha and Tasha shrugged at each other. Then Tasha grabbed hold of Aidan and the seven of them made their way out onto the terrace running the length of the pub. They crept to the end of it, then

Philly signalled to them to stop. She peered round the corner, then she stood back and motioned to Sean to look.

Sean stepped forward and craned round the wall. 'Yes – YES!' he breathed ecstatically. 'C'mere – *look*!' He beckoned frantically to the others. Silently everyone crept to the corner and peered round.

The terrace continued round the corner for a couple of metres and at the end of it was a wooden bench under a bower of what would have been roses in the summer. On the bench, heedless of the cold, sat Joel, legs sprawled out in front of him, eyes blissfully closed. And lying half across him, elegantly arranged, lay Karina.

'Oh, blimey,' muttered Tasha, happily. 'Oh, this is great. This is *so – oo* good.'

'Joel's found someone,' said Aisha, linking her arm through Ness's. 'We're safe, Ness. He's found someone dumb enough to take him on.'

'Go, Karina,' whispered Ness 'Go, *girl*!'

Unaware of her audience for once, Karina sat up a little, and smiled at Joel. He opened his eyes and smiled back. 'I mean – I dunno, Joel,' she said, 'I just really think if anyone's going to make it – I mean any of us – it's going to be me or you.'

'Me *and* you,' gurgled Joel. 'Let's both make it.'

Karina giggled shrilly and gave his chest a push. 'I'm being serious, here, Joel!' she squeaked. 'I mean make it in *acting*! The others just aren't committed, are they? Not like we are.'

Joel took hold of one of her hands and pressed it to his lips. Sean ducked back round the corner and started choking. '*Shhhh*!' warned Tasha.

'No one's like you Karina,' slurred Joel. 'Seriously. You're one of the best actresses I've ever seen. If you'd been playing Sandy . . .'

Karina wound her arms gracefully around Joel's neck. 'Yee – es . . . ?' she said.

'. . . we could really have set the stage on fire.'

That did it. The whole group collapsed helpless with laughter, just as Joel was moving in for a major smooch. Sean and Ian started clapping loudly, shouting, 'Encore! Encore!'

Karina shot to her feet, spitting fire. 'You lot are just so *PATHETIC*!' she screeched. 'You're like a lot of *KIDS*. Have you *REALLY* got nothing better to *DO* with your time?'

Still laughing, Tasha laced her fingers through Aidan's, and Ian pulled Philly towards him. Aisha waved happily and headed indoors, summoned by the loud music. 'Yeah,' said Sean, wrapping his arms round Ness with a grin, 'I think maybe we have. A *lot* better!'